HERTS IN PIECES

THE HERTFORDSHIRE WRITING GROUP

CALUM DICKINSON   TAYLOR MCLEOD

EMILY SIGGERS   ALEXANDRA DIACONESCU

BERNADETTE LYNN   CÉCILE KEEN

CONTENTS

Just Another Cog   1
by Calum Dickinson

A Little Ball of Sadness   25
by Cécile Keen

Pig 108239   41
by Taylor Mcleod

Shooting Stars   81
by Cécile Keen

Life's a Stage   99
by Bernadette Lynn

I Am Strong   125
by Alexandra Diaconescu

A Fresh Start   129
by Emily Siggers

Afterword   171

About the Authors   173

Also by The Group   177

JUST ANOTHER COG
BY CALUM DICKINSON

ALL RESOURCES ARE FINITE! A chant that almost became a prayer when we said it as one. The purple glow danced in the mirror, bouncing off my teeth. It sucked a wider smile from me as air whistled through the toothy gaps. Fuzziness tingled through my fingers, tiny pins and needles. Teeny weeny blue sparks would arc sometimes. The little blue gremlins clawed at me as I tugged a wire from the carcass of the old bot. That last grip on life before the now defunct was melted down. The heap of scrap dropped to the floor, waiting for the command to the Shufflers to unclutter the work-booth. Nothing went to waste on this line. Every chip and wire counted for the daily haul and, more importantly, my quota. The UV light thrummed like that throb behind your eyes. The beam guarding any light-sensitive parts from harm. One wrong glare, and the sensors would be useless and this shift would have been for nothing.

Only one harmful glare was at me now, though. My booth mate and the sneer he sent across to me. The spark was like a drug to me, and his nose crinkle of disgust was clear. I stared back in a fugue state, almost challenging him to "dob me in" as we used to say on the playground. Always attempting to get that strike on my record for skipping out on the PPE. *Personal Protective Equipment - the ability to turn your entire body into one giant thumb!* The Thick Suits! The Gloves! The Goggles! The Masks! They were meant to protect, keep out the nasties. The Shocks! The Fumes! The Sharps! It smothered everything. IT SMOTHERED EVERYTHING!

Cut off the feeling of metal on my skin, dulling my moves. Slowing me down, making me feel clumsy, making me blunt as the butterknife of my booth mate plodding through quotas. Without it, steam never fogged my view. No goggles blurred the fine tracks of a circuit board. I could catch that sharp tang of the leaking battery straight away. That acidic scratch at the back of my throat, a warning before disaster striking. I was faster than any alarm, saving a whole batch from ruin just last week, by pitching a damaged cell before even a drop of acid hit the floor.

How could I be expected to use sausages to delicately twist out a component? I will leave those gloves well alone. I couldn't spin a microscrew or nudge the little pin switch into place. They would steal the edge that I had, and I needed that sharpness. I was the quickest in my booth, which, to be honest, was nothing to shout about, considering who my booth mate was. Fastest on the line though, that was for sure. Likely even the entire floor, even if it had more stations than I could care to count. My quotas always hit in half the time that it took others. I'd always finish my stack early, then eye up the extras. The howl of the slower projects would beckon me forward. Lower risk... smaller payoffs... no big bonuses – still, the reward for me, that was priceless. It beat the monotony of the day, my hands reaching for that dance among the parts, keeping them alive amid the finite nature of my surroundings.

That vital chip! Spot it before anyone else, and grab it like your life depended on it. That one small step for another bot's path to the factory line, one giant leap up a rank for you. Everyone would hustle for those. Focus on tweaking the shield plates instead, blocking the solar flares and blasts of radiation that could fry a Repair-bot's circuits. Nail the shields, gain an early clock out from the bosses. No thankless, unpaid overtime trapping you in the scrap pile, circling your disposal chute like your productivity score. Then, my favourite, the minor tasks. Pecking at the plastic bits stuck on a circuit board, a tangled nest of wires or carefully meshing together a plumage of parts that only once combined gained purpose. Someone had to do these tasks. The low scrap levels would keep the conveyors running smoothly, never enough to pay your bill, to brag about what you found or climb the ladder out of the line. And yet, it was these oddities that would capture me. In a world that tremored with rumbling belts, I caught on fast that the quick rewards were on top, and it was the satisfaction that slid down to the lowest spots.

Deep down in the depths of the conveyor troughs, down where screws vibrated, belts undulated, and metal filings mingled with dust. A location as alien to high-value items as a productive booth mate was to me. My hands would dive in, past the survival of the fastest hands region, past the big win of the strong hands area, past the "let's cross our fingers and hope for the best" plateau. They swirled today through the mess of wires and the metal shards. Each minor cut, insignificant on its own, but together making me wish I had put on the sharps gloves. Numbing fingers on the edge of paralysis, hovering at the boundary of pain meeting promise. The regret evaporating quickly as I grasped that feeling that I had reached treasure. Pulling that one little gem from the abyss of tangled parts. A steady pulse of light initially blinked back at me, or more like winking at me as if the little module wanted to congratulate me for finding it. It hummed with potential, even in the world of making behemoths that could block out a star that mocked us with the inevitable.

Now, of course, I know that I should have returned that little bot to the trough of discarded dreams. My eyes met the goggles of the 'lumbering one of the booth', his sneer contorting his face like an earthworm in water. My little booth gremlin, with his know-it-all spark, daring me to do the forbidden action of returning something. And yet, there was also the curiosity, it clawed deeply at me, pointedly and stroking my body, raising the skin to an itch that you cannot ignore. The desire to take a quick peek at what may be the reason for the flashing. Deep down, I should have known better. I should have discarded it to the floor for the Shuffler and take the strike. I did know better, and yet, the current spinning objects above me are the repercussions for casting away better judgement.

I used to be the highest performer on the line, even on the entire floor. I could replay that moment over and over again in my head. No excuses. We would not be where we are today or even where I am if I had made a better choice. The lingering stale air of my booth haunts that memory, although that may have just been my stinking booth mate!

1100011101111011100011001110001111001

As you can probably gather, I work at my booth in the disassembly plant. I cannot always tell if the hum of the machines is through my ears or my feet. All the discarded components are constantly flowing by like the dead in the fetid river Styx. If every blinking light stopped me in my tracks, then my output would be worse than the moss-covered stone that is my booth mate. And that is saying something. The light was not the reason that I paused. A blinking light simply meant that I was reaching for my trusty old rust covered magnet. A quick swipe, and that pesky residual data would be gone, unable to corrupt the next bot. Nobody wanted a bot that would glitch out. Build a bot that could save the world, build it reusing the parts of those that came before it. Then the tiniest of slithers, still with a charge of old cold, is stuck inside. That bot becomes rotten, it starts to fail and we may as well just pin a tail on those smart programmers, as they're gonna be chasing that code on the bot like their own tail! So, we demagnetise, and we demagnetise fast. Strip it out and push it along the line. Reach for that next part and repeat. Otherwise, Chaos just runs amok.

So, it was not the light that stopped me, it was the odd rhythm. It was not a steady blink. Sometimes quick bursts. Other times, there was a longer, slower pulse that felt lethargic. This was not a simple ready light, it was something more! It reminded me of the archaic messages sent by soldiers across a battlefield. Short flashes, long flashes and a pattern. There was definitely a pattern. And it repeated after a pause.

I rolled the little bot in my hand as it kept signalling. You had to watch it close to see how it was repeating. I had pulled this bot from the dark clutches of oblivion, from the despair that the message that was the purpose of the signal was never going to be seen. The bot did not realise that the one who pulled it from the junk was deaf to its call, or rather blind to it.

11110011001010000100010000111110001

Now, I would just like to make myself clear. This bot held no shape of a puppy. Nothing about the bot, or even the likely tasks that it may have been designed for, hinted at any canine-like tendencies. I decided to refer to it as a Puppy Bot because as it sat in my hand, it reminded me of the litter of my childhood dog, and how each puppy nestled in my hand, all warm and helpless. The Puppy Bot was not just some simple gadget with a lone blinking light. Yes, it came from old tech, and as my thumb brushed against the port at the side, I realised I had no means to observe it. The port matched my viewing screen, something I used for assessing the hard drives fished from the troughs. Before we could use these hard drives, they needed to be data checked before wiping, depending on what we found.

If any scraps of data were found, then they would be flagged on the screen. If no flag was raised, I would run the magnet over for good measure. We had to keep those ghosts out of those bots. If data was still intact, then we had to hand it over. It was someone else's job to track the sloppy worker who was too lazy to wipe. Follow that official protocol and trace the leak back to where it came from, and with that, the culprit would be getting a nasty surprise.

Unofficially? There was absolutely no chance I was going to let this cold, dead, mechanical planet chew anyone up and spit out what's left. Yes, the person should not have done it, but if I was willing to hand it over, then I would be as slimy as my slug-like booth mate. So, I kept quiet, the magnet did the job, and those drives went on to better protect the planet.

I pulled out my viewer from under my workstation. Dust clung to the edges, and it started to rejoin the world of the living as the screen booted up. The viewer cable was inserted into Puppy Bot, and a small plume of dust puffed out as the viewer kicked in. That little screen worked hard, as I could feel it flicking through the internal memory banks trying to decipher the language of Puppy Bot and the outdated code. The search for the matching language that would make sense of the Puppy Bot's secrets was on.

If I had known what waited, I would have pulled that cable out right there and then. Snatch it free before that connection was properly established. Curiosity held me still. Curiosity fixed my eyes on the screen. Curiosity watched the text come in. Those sharp words that caused my world to freeze.

1110000100010001111011011100111

CONFIRM... YES OR NO

1110110110001000111000110111110101

I let a sharp huff out through my nose. With all the clanging of the machinery surrounding us, you would think that it would not make a difference. The tsk from my booth mate said otherwise, as my reflection stared back from his goggles. I fired a stare back at him, I felt it was weak, but it was enough for him to turn away. My stare lacked form, yet that question from Puppy was strong. I waited for the next prompt to flash up. Anything... at least it should give me something... instead it just loaded up the same question on the next line.

CONFIRM... YES OR NO

And what did it even matter? This bot was long gone, function gone as it trundled along the conveyor belt, forgotten. That signal, just an apparition in the wires. A leftover program that had continued to tick along, powered by a dodgy battery or some residual solar bank. How long had it even been in the trough? Making loop upon loop upon loop past me. Was it months? Years? Hard to say. No outer sensors to pick up the passage of time. No internal sensors to take note that it was not being answered. Puppy was just a metal shell, barking out that faint little signal into a debris ridden world. Broadcasting out a call that no one cared about. And just like my booth mate, no brain to know whether someone heard and no heart to feel the silence that came back.

The cursor blinked at me from the viewer. Steady. Mocking. Taunting. The rhythm without rhyme to Puppy's weak pulsing signal. The blinking repeated pattern, completely different from the clocklike tick of the cursor that dared me to continue, to answer the question. I could not answer it, though. I physically could not. Even if I understood the question, I had no means of answering. The question stayed as a puzzle, out of reach for me. The viewer only let me read the question, that was all. No keys to type back. No way to tap yes or no. I felt sorry for Puppy. It was endlessly looping this message out for so long for it to be tripped up by my not knowing how to respond. The fool — that was the only thing between Puppy and that big magnet on my hip.

My hand moved on autopilot, reaching for the magnet. It was protocol. Cold and clear protocol. I had spotted the data signalling out. I confirmed it with my viewer. It was now time to wipe it clean. Scrub those echoes right out of Puppy's hair. Keep that waste code from ghosting up the next bot. No loose wires to spark trouble later.

"What are you doing there, Howland?"
1101000111010010100011110110111
The sudden voice ran a shock down my spine. The jolt travelled through my guilt as I grabbed Puppy and thrust it into my dungarees. The pull was rough, maybe too rough, as Puppy's cable tail got pulled from the viewer. The tiny hope that I had not caused any lasting damage. Only my supervisor ever called me Howland, the shape of my surname hanging in the air accusingly. I spun around to the

little gnat that was a constant buzz of annoyance, the likely source of the report of my behaviour. Gone! An empty seat! He stirs the pot and then bolts with his tail between his legs, leaving me to scoop up the mess.

"I was just checking a drive!" I blurted out. The words cascaded across the floor, which is nearly what happened with the screen and magnet as I pushed them with shaking hands towards my supervisor.

Confusion contorted his face for a second, with brows knitting together above the pearls of his eyes. "I can see that much. Look at the clock! Get yourself home already!"

I glanced up at the clock. The tick told me the shift ended ages ago, and the tock mocked me for ignoring it in the dim light. A fog had settled in my head, the night enveloping me. It felt only minutes ago, the sun had blazed high overhead heating the protective windows. Puppy's light had dragged me in. No time to dig in my nails, just sucked into the trap of thought. The question posed seemed so basic. A yes or no, nothing more. Truth is, I did not need to answer it at all. I could have tossed it back into the trough and let it continue on the circuit tour around me. Puppy already had its fair share of dust. It was not as if he could dock me points, my shift tallies would have my daily quota covered from earlier that day.

"Clocking off now, Sir!" I managed, forcing out a brief nod.

"See that you do. The later that you punch out, the worse your score drops."

He turned on his heel, clanging boots echoing back towards me as he strode off. No backward glance of reproach. Nothing about breaking rules or taking Puppy into my pocket. Was it the guilt that twisted my trembling stomach or simply Puppy, the wriggle of internal workings faint against my ribs? Tiny little motors whining — showing that there was still life, or simply my mind playing tricks?

11101010001000100010000100010111

ALL RESOURCES ARE FINITE! Our Mantra! Our Chant! Our Prayer! Every part had to get reused. This rule wove the very fabric of our new society. The backbone of the new world order that we had scraped back from the ruins. Before the nations collapsed, before they had burned through everything they had. Easy come, easy go. Harder to come, easy to go. No more to come, now we must go. We knew it, we still chose to squander it, and our future paid for it.

Those who survived learned fast. The countries that made it through the shortages rationed everything as the others tried breaking more of our fragile earth. Wars erupted as the strive for more was everywhere. Force did not win, though. It backfired. The attackers sent missiles across the skies, bombs dropped from planes and drones. The defenders? They salvaged it all. The shells melted into tools, into wires, into circuits. Every aggressive action lost the attacker more than it could gain. No more pulling of underground riches. All long gone, stripped bare, now mixed in the massive toxic dumps that no one could touch. Nothing could be brought back from that time — all useless sludge. Those broken nations could meander through the old wrecks, a graveyard of their former home.

We used to fear the bombs. That it would be the war that would end us. Or that unknown pathogen, that invisible enemy, that we would be powerless against. No, none of that. It was our plain and raw greed. We filled our bellies until bursting. We did not care then. We wasted it all, from soil to sky, until we got the last bill. In this new world, we reuse or we starve. Every bolt, every wire. We salvage, we sort, and it is reborn. Puppy in my pocket? That little bot will get stripped tomorrow, the parts – a new cog in our great societal machine. *That is the cost! That is the value! We will survive!*

11101000100010010111110101011010101

I pulled Puppy from my dungarees pocket when I was alone in my tiny cubit. My space was bare, no need for decorations. Just walls, a bed and a sink. All built for efficiency to rule, no room for extras. The quiet could hit hard, though. Gone were the rumbles and clanks from the shop floor. My mind had no choice but to fill the gaps with noises that did not exist. Was that a whisper of wind? A distant hum? Footsteps? It tricked me constantly. The giant silent roar in my head.

The choice paid off for me, though. I saved everything I could. No waste in comfort, no lost rent on unneeded space. My wages piled high, and this preparation kept me ahead. Not everyone saw it that way. They took the same pay home. They ignored the company's Cubit, which was basic and safe. They would set up outside the complex. Risky areas with fear of death from wild animals or suffocation from the wrong air. All of this for the same wage. No bonus for being brave or rather stupid. It is no surprise what path my booth mate took. Completely excessive with a multi-room domicile. Space to lounge around, to entertain guests, even a table to eat meals. Useless and wasteful! Something I did not crave. The bed serves me well. It can free up the funds to buy out my indenture. Then, I would get real freedom. My dreams sparked at the thought.

I flipped the cold metal of Puppy over in my palm. No labels, no movements. Just that blinking light, that same blinking pattern. I had no viewer to see what it meant. I knew, though. "CONFIRM...YES OR NO". That pause between the two groups of blinks. A clear split. First, for the command. Second, for the choice. A choice that I was unable to answer. I made up my mind, Puppy was going to meet a magnet tomorrow. It was not the end for Puppy. In this new world, there was no death, only a simple shift. A new life. A new purpose.

110001001111001101001101101101011

My hands were a whirl. The goal of my quota loomed. I chased it down, quick. Movements, precise. Fluid. A chasse in dance. Not the dragging and trudging of my booth mate's shuffle. Heavy shame burned through me like a guilty kangaroo as I smuggled Puppy like another's joey. One slip, and the secret would tumble out. All eyes would watch as I fumbled for it. I intended to throw Puppy back in, or slag it. The light flickering off the goggles of my booth mate's scrutiny stopped that. He threw me off my stride, and I realised from the weight of the item I picked; it was a mistake. My fingers had gripped the wrong part. That rat tail dragging behind it only meant one thing. A go-slow item. Old tech. Mainly plastic. Only fools grabbed those, and normally on purpose. Risk getting booted out. Low yield and likely a way to stick it to the company on your way out.

My booth mate snorted, turning away at the pick. He did not need to watch every minute, he knew I would be at this for a couple of hours. If it disappeared, well, he would know what I did. Wait! A spark hit me. This was an input device and that cable. Maybe. Yes, that cable could connect to the viewer. Could I send an answer back to Puppy? I could feel the blink through the thick dungaree fabric. Demanding that I give the question what it craved. An answer!

1010011101110001100011010101011011

I should have drawn my magnet from my holster straight away. That simple tool could have erased everything in seconds. Wipe Puppy clean, strip its circuits bare before it had turned into a problem. But no. When my booth mate stepped out for his break, I got curious. I hooked up the input device straight to the viewer screen, a little wheel rotated as the viewer searched for how to accept the input. Puppy once again was presented to my breakdown desk, and his tail once more inserted into the viewer. The viewer would need to search once more for the language. I was ready, though, for that question. It was on a loop, I knew what it would ask, and I did not have to wait too long. Presenting once more, bold and insistent.

CONFIRM... YES OR NO?

Did Puppy ever get frustrated? Looping the same question over and over again? The processor salivating. Tugging against the constraints of the leash. My finger hovered over the Y key, tense. My eyes locked on the N. A slight tremble. What difference did it make? I had no clue what the question meant. I had no clue whether, even with the confirmation of the command, the defunct bot could take action. Frustration built inside me, and hoping for clarity, I jabbed at the D key.

DEFINE WHAT TO BE CONFIRMED?

Was that command too simple? Too vague? I did not know how "Smart" Puppy was. Did it simply follow orders? Could it adapt to change? Would I have to work out a list of commands rather than use sentences? The simple request was processed, and the viewer flickered.

It shot back:

CONFIRM... YES

Then:

CONFIRM... NO

And then, as if overpowered by that original route, it circled back:

CONFIRM... YES OR NO

Regret can hit hard. I should have wiped Puppy then. I should have pulled out every wire, cleaved off every chip when I had that chance. When you are in your booth, you learn to do things fast. A quick running over with a magnet and the memory would be scrambled. The question forgotten. The end of Puppy. Instead, it was the end of the break of my booth mate. Seeing him suddenly appear approaching the booth, I panicked and tapped the Y key.

111101001101001110001001001001010101

SHUTDOWN INITIATED

110100111000100010001001010010100

Puppy's lights dimmed. A silence fell from the ceiling like a shroud. Metal still clanked away. The wheels of the conveyor still squeaked as they trundled along. Yet, the pressure of the soundless felt oppressive. The familiar blinking light, a pursuit of an answer that Puppy was always chasing, was gone. The end felt flat. Too easy. I had not realised what was about to follow.

A low purr began from inside Puppy. It built, turning into a growl that reverberated through the table. An increase in speed, a shriller tone, piercing as whatever was spinning intensified. Panic surged through me, and it was not my holster I went for. Instead, it was the hammer. The blunt instrument of destruction that was used to break open the harder cases or move those stubborn fittings. We rarely tried to destroy. We had to save, not sacrifice. The pitch climbed higher, slicing through the air with a slashing whine. Heads turned to try to trace the source as workers paused, eyes scanning. The noise bounced off all the structures, both walls and apparatus alike. Everyone knew what the noise meant. Everyone knew it meant that there was trouble brewing. Hands went on ears, grimaces all around as the screech tried to rip out their brains.

My hammer slammed down... it slammed...it... it stopped inches away. Frozen by some invisible barrier. Meeting a force strong, unyielding, and one that pushed back. I'd felt this before. When trying to force two magnets together. Poles repelling. Puppy should not be sending out a magnetic force like this. That sort of magnetism would wipe its own circuits. That's why we kept magnets around for removing the bad code. And my hammer? That was standard steel, no magnetic pull at all. None of this made sense to me. Beads started to form on my brow as I stared at Puppy. What had I unleashed?

1010010010000100111100010101100111

My magnet. In my holster. There was still time to stop this. Scramble Puppy's brain before disaster struck. What sort of disaster I did not know, but I hoped that I did not need to find out. My hand gripping the hammer was useless. Paralysed in mid-air. Unable to let go. Unable to pull back. Unable to follow through. Just that steady thrum pulsing up my arm, as if a live wire. My free hand reached round my body, fingers settling on the magnet's handle. I swung it around towards Puppy. Ripples shot through me. That same repelling force clamping down. Both arms paralysed, stuck out front. Rigid. Useless.

A screech ripped up from the conveyor belts. They shuddered, grinding to a halt with a final whine along the entire line. Lights did not go out in sequence like when the factory switches went off. They just stopped, vanishing all at once. Plunging everything into that inky blackness. Puppy was silent. The sudden quiet from the machines felt like I was deafened. I could still feel my ears ringing. Then came clattering, the unsteady metal parts starting to topple over, no longer held steady with the momentum of the belt. In the dark, something shifted. Tens...no, hundreds... of tiny little lights started to flicker, scattered around like fireflies. The leftover spark, the residuals from old bots. Nothing new. I had seen it before. The disturbing part though was that they were all blinking the same thing, a unified glow that chilled me.

I glanced at the blinking cursor on the viewer, brighter in the darkness of the factory. Words appeared.

REBOOT ACTIVATED

11101010011101101001110001111001010

The whirr had faded the moment everything powered down. It had felt like hours that constant and steady hum had filled my ears, a remaining echo from the machines. Puppy released my hands, the hammer and magnet suddenly feeling like great weights, and clattered to the floor. Lights returned, blinding me after I had grown accustomed to the dark. Through a blur, I wondered if there was time to stop this. I typed EXIT into the input device.

The cursor jumped to the next line. Flashing off and on. Puppy paid no attention to the command. Had the connection been severed when powered down? Or was it simply an unrecognised command? What had I started? Why did I need to click the Y? My gut churned at the thought of what was likely happening without me realising it. I dropped that interface and ran out of the booth. Health and safety signs flashed at me to walk and not run. I have ignored those rules plenty of times in my life, and most of that was out of pure laziness. I always had to get there and back with a tool in record time. Now, it was not being lazy, it reeked of fear.

Rules existed for a reason. I vaulted down the stairs, missing three steps. Trip hazards lay everywhere on the floor of the disassembly plant. My boots clanged against the walkway. Loose cables wound around the floor, and scattered parts left by the Shufflers waited to catch your boot. I twisted round the corner, yanking the bannister as I took it at speed. One slip could end you. Even in light, I could see the sparks leaping out from the conveyor belt as the bots began to rise. My foot caught something sharp. Statistics of how many falls had happened this year flashed through my mind. I launched forward, the air whizzing past me. New sparks erupted as my head cracked against the railing on the way down. Hard metal snapping my neck back. The shadows of the standing bots, travelling along the conveyors as if they marched, were dimming.

11010010010001001111101010101011

I stir as the cold floor presses against my cheek. How much time has passed? Minutes or hours? I have no clue, but something was now lifting me. Carrying me. Strapping me to a table, pinning my arms. The whirring, it was back. Not Puppy, or any of the other Residual bots. Not this time. This whirr was closer, very mechanical, very precise. Tiny drills spinning on extended arms. Rotating saws coming in from the side. Very close to my skin now, the cold teeth about to bit. I am looking past the tools, and I can only see that one phrase, burned in red letters.

11101101101101110001101001 0110....2

In a world where every bolt, every wire, every electronic chip and every drop of oil counted. Every life counted as stock. In this new world, there was no death, only a simple shift. A new life. A new purpose.

ALL RESOURCES ARE FINITE!

A LITTLE BALL OF SADNESS
BY CÉCILE KEEN

There is a *Little Ball of Sadness* alive inside of me.

I never invited it and still don't welcome it.

I cannot remember exactly when it chose me. As to why it did, there's no point searching for the answer anymore. All I know, is that I was young. Too young to comprehend what was happening, too young to explain how I was feeling and too young to ask for help.

I thought it would go away on its own accord.

It did not.

It had decided to stay, long before I realised I needed it to go.

When I was five years old, Mummy started to worry about my tantrums over seemingly tiny things. I would sulk, then whine and scream whilst flailing my arms. Most of the time, I would end up hiding under the dining table, drowning in my own tears. No-one could reason with me. Mummy was calm and patient, but despite her words of encouragement, I would stay in this state of anguish to the point of exhaustion until sleep gave us both relief. Once Mummy finally recognised my crying was beyond any normal acceptable childhood upsets, she took me to see someone. The Lady said I could talk to her about anything, and it was between me and her. She was lovely. She listened to me, especially when I was silent. She let me cry. Never told me to *"stop for God's sake"*, like Daddy did. On the little table in her office, next to the Winnie-the-Pooh tissue box, was a cube. Each side had a smiley face drawn on it, though half of them were a fraud to their name since they were not smiling at all. The Lady encouraged me to turn the cube to display on top the face that better suited my frame of mind at the time. I could also change it throughout our chat together. But even at a young age, I knew whatever this was, it was far too complex to be reduced to six isolated faces smiling or not.

The Lady advised naming my sorrow would help control it. So, I called it *"The Little Ball of Sadness"* because it is how it felt at the beginning: just a little something that rolled inside me making everything gloomy and blue. It made sweets salty and playing outside the hardest challenge one could imagine. No cuddles from Mummy could make it better.

The *Little Ball* was cleverer than us all. It sought much more than just rolling about. From the very day it found me, its purpose was to install itself permanently, and it knew how to do it. First, it found its birth in my heart and then travelled through my body, attaching a tiny bit of itself onto every single cell of my being, as if marking its territory with overwhelming might. Then, it settled and built a home in my stomach, in between my chest and navel, right in the middle of my belly. If I rest my hand on my tummy, where it resides, I can almost feel its round malicious shape despite the flatness of my skin, that reveals nothing undesirable.

The Lady helped stop the *Ball* from growing too much. We met every week until I had what she called "a toolbox" to help deal with things.

My teenage years registered many good days, but I took to release the darkness in bloody ways hidden under long-sleeved tops. It felt exhilarating to be in control at last. A few razor lines were sufficient to silence the *Little Ball*, not permanently but for a while anyway. However, once healed, the scars still exposed me to shame and fear of judgment. At

18 years old, I found a way to hide my sins: an appointment at the tattoo studio gave me a new lease of life. The flowers and butterfly inked on my arms by the tattoo artist symbolised just that: renewal. Not wanting to destroy the design on my arms, I started on the inside of my thighs. Somehow, it never rewarded me with the similar release. Looking back, the habit fading away coincided with moving from home to university to do what I loved.

The joy of studying Mathematics is like no other. It is an intellectual challenge that relies on analysis and logic. Because Maths can be explained, it can be understood. It is not subjective nor dependent on opinions or feelings. Our lives are reliant on maths: from our mobile phone, the most advanced medical procedures that save lives, the construction of our homes to space exploration. All are built on mathematical principles. Numbers do not fail us because they are solid and objective. They work the same from one day to the next. They do not surprise us. Instead, they give us rules to follow and by doing so, they provide strength and stability.

These days at university were the best, filled with learning, friends, fun and new experiences. My graduation in Mathematics followed by the completion of a PhD and the stepping through the expected joyful adult milestones made everyone forget about the *Little Ball*.

The *Ball* had not forgotten me though and had not vacated its comfortable premises. It was biding its time, waiting for a comeback with greater strength. When it did, it was as sly as a professional con artist: it used the memory of wonderful days to dupe me into trusting they would be back. That's why the *Ball* felt innocuous, almost unremarkable at first. I should have known better. When it started to weigh slightly more in my tummy, I persuaded myself I was too stressed, too busy, too bored, too tired, too whatever. My work was too demanding; I should apply for this new interesting senior role; I was eating too much, I was not eating enough; I needed time for myself, I needed time with the children. No doubt somehow life will be easier soon, and of course the *Little Ball* would go away.

Slowly good days became tainted, spoiled, polluted. It was all a game for the *Ball*, because it had nothing to lose. Gradually, it staked out its claim again to what once used to be mine. It enrolled its allies amongst the rain, the darkness of winter, and the gloom of starless nights. For me, who felt alone and did not understand fully the rules of the game, victory had yet to come but I could still win battles.

Nowadays, the *Little Ball* is never small enough to

be forgotten. Sometimes, it is small enough to be ignored, but it is always here.

Always here.

Never ever gone.

Even for the shortest of moments.

Now, I have come to know its insidious ways and how it slivers in. It is a quiet passenger that is forever loitering and lurking for an opportunity to mutate into a parasite. It then latches on to my happiness and on any piece of joy my spirit is capable of. It paints fog onto my eyes and holds me prisoner in a straitjacket of such coldness, that it erodes any sense of touch from my toes to my fingertips. It deafens my ears with its shouting, against which the best ear defenders would offer no protection. It has trans-formed me into a weak and quiet being; me, who used to be the merry soul of parties with friends. These same friends could not even recognise me anymore. It has silenced both my voice and appetite for such a long time, that the memory of enjoying a meal escapes me. It makes me doubt the sunshine on the warmest of summer days. If I am not careful, it could take away so much more than I dare say.

Sometimes the *Little Ball* allows me to be. Well, to just be.

1, 2, 3, 4: Wash, Dress, Breakfast, School run

5, 6, 7: Clean, Cook, School run

8, 9, 10: Dinner, TV, Bed

Here is my compressed and organised routine, the ten vital components of my survival kit. Keeping afloat despite the crushing waves of an ocean of desperation is no easy task. Each of the ten steps is a robust anchor securing my stability. Pythagoras believed that 10 is a symbol of perfection, completeness and wholeness. Numbers are consistent and dependable. They are not subject to change because they are fixed values. I can hold on to these ten numbers. They will not forsake me.

The *Ball* may have stolen my career but not my confidence in numbers. For the mathematics professor that I was, they strengthen the hope to return to my whole self. Numbers do not lie. They reveal factually two things: one is what has been achieved and two is what still lays ahead. Numbers pull me forward; each one is a winning step. These ten numbers form the path, along which I can gather the broken pieces of myself to put back together.

They mean I can do it by following the ten steps.

I can do it if I focus.

I really can do it …

… if the *Ball* behaves that is, of course.

I am on step 4 right now, driving and on the way back home from school. I had been feeling calm and collected until the radio plays what should simply be a beautiful romantic song. The *Ball* has other ideas though. It seizes every single note of the melancholic tune and gorges itself silly on it. The rich mellow piano notes, the smooth depth of the violins, the singer's soft voice, the meaningful lyrics. All of it - individually and collectively - empower the *Ball* to grow uncontrollably. Wildly, it starts swirling, whirling and twirling in my stomach, spewing its venom all over and inside me, overwhelming me with its taste of disease in my mouth. Is it too late for me? I fear it might be, since I am losing my already weak grip. I must battle on, nonetheless.

"Crash the car into the trees", it whispers to me.

"It's quick and easy"

"All will stop, no more pain", it cajoles.

"It's worth it"

"Come on, it will look like something went wrong with car", it encourages.

Oh, the sweet temptation of giving in.

There is no point turning the radio off. I know that from experience.

Instead, I slap my own cheeks repeatedly and sing out loud to the song. It's a trick I learnt to distract my ears.

The *Ball* is still in charge though. At this point, it is hard to tell when it will cease to be in command. And that, I know from experience too. Who can guess how long the song will be enough nourishment to sustain its power? In the past, on one occasion, it had refused to leave me alone. It destroyed me with emotions, that ruled everything in my life. When, in my weakest moment, I questioned the worth of battling on in a war that may never end, I took action to terminate my unbearable agony. After waking up on a hospital bed, horrified by what I had done, I endured weeks stuck in a miserable ward, before the *Ball* finally released me from its clutches, a feeble and drained shadow of myself, almost too ghostly to exist amongst the living. My enemy never tires. It only granted a respite to play with the boneless doll I had become, again and again and again. What is the fun in an unresponsive opponent? So, it released me and waited for me to regain some strength, only to resume its Machiavellian game at its own leisure.

"It won't even hurt" it starts again

"Or just close your eyes, if you prefer"

"Take your hands off the steering wheel", it commands.

No more battling. Silence, Peace and Freedom at last.

I am holding on to the song and keep singing out loud lyrics I don't really know. So, I am making words up. They make no sense but at least they silence the poisoned voice somewhat. When the last notes of the song are playing on the radio, will the

Ball begin to deflate? Maybe I am too tough a rival to defeat this time. I would like that. It would soothe me if I could still have a say in my destiny.

But mercy is alien to the *Little Ball*. Instead, the battle reinvigorates its malice.

"You're not wanted" it says loudly

No-one could want someone like me.

"You're not needed"

Who really needs me?

"You won't be missed" it screams in my ears

What's the point of me?

The *Ball* is right. It is not difficult, so easy to do this time.

I could close my eyes now. Sleep for a second and then forever.

I am about to let go when the radio presenter cheerfully announces:

"Happy 4th Birthday Evie. Mummy, Daddy and big Sis love you very much and send you lots of kisses" followed by the traditional "Happy Birthday song".

Four years old? Have I heard right?

Four years old, just like my sweet little one. My oldest is only 6. The reflection of the two empty booster seats in the rearview mirror snatches me out of my submissive torpor.

What if the girls were in the car too right now?

This one question deafened my ears.

I turn left into a discount supermarket carpark and drive towards the far end, away from everyone.

I breathe in and I breathe out.

Slowly.

I was warned. One more episode in the hospital and the girls would be taken away into care. As a widow, I am the sole responsible parent. If I cannot be trusted in that role, then the State will be on my behalf.

"Just pull yourself together" the social worker had said. As if it was that easy. Not everyone is lucky enough to have family around. My father is estranged, and my mother has dementia. As for my husband, he would want to be here. Life would have been completely different with him around, but fate has decided otherwise. So, I am alone in this. Since the usual family network is non-existent, the *Little Ball* has plenty to feed on and grow. I am the perfect prey.

I switch the car engine off and stay where I am parked.

I breathe in and I breathe out.

My closed eyes remember and show me: the children's births, the birthday parties, the games in the garden, the sound of their laughter, the touch of their puffy soft baby hands, the smell of their hair when they fall asleep in my arms.

They are my most precious, gorgeous clever little angels. I love their cute dimples when they smile and the shine in their eyes when they are mischievous and conspiring together. Yesterday only, the youngest attempted to distract me, whilst the oldest helped herself to a few sweets from the cupboard. I pretended not to know what they were up to. They ran back to their bedroom giggling happily, delighted in their fruitful team effort. It felt so good to see they had not inherited a *Little Ball* of their own.

What I need is very specific happy memories, they prevent my mind from wandering. The *Ball* doesn't like them. I pick up my mobile phone, touch the photo icon, then select the folder entitled "Real Happiness". Hundreds of photos saved over time and in no particular order are stored:

The front cover of "Principia" by Newton. I have not read it for a while but have many times before. Perhaps I will fetch it from the bookshelf once I am home.

The local park in October. Looking at the autumn rusty leaves hanging on to the branches against a bright blue sky, I can almost feel the refreshing crispness of the cold on my cheeks.

The photo of my doctorate graduation. My academic gown could not be defined as fetching or fashionable, but God did I look good and rightly proud in it!

Of course, there are many photos of my girls. Some are when they are playing and serving tea to a range of well-behaved teddies. Others are close up and the girls are aware I am taking pictures: grinning smiles with missing teeth or funny poses. The one that stops me from scrolling any further is a photo of the girls blowing kisses at me and forming a heart with their fingers.

The *Ball* cannot have my girls.

And it cannot take me away from them either.

Never.

The photos have done their job. They helped bring me back to reality enough for me to follow the grounding technique my therapist taught me. It is designed to re-focus on the present moment. 5-4-3-2-1. Five things I can see. Four things I can feel. Three I can hear, Two I can touch and One I can taste.

I work with these five numbers. They work with me and for me reliably, unfailingly and worthy of my trust. Time has become unimportant. Numbers again save me and bring me back to the present, showing me life is worth living. They help me realise I am not stuck in a black hole. There is joy in simple everyday things. Moments of happiness surround me, always and all the time, it is just a question of stopping my own thoughts to acknowledge them. The numbers guide me to notice them:

The mum chatting and laughing with her baby in the shopping trolley as they enter the supermarket.

The drifting smell of fresh coffee, that the wind carries along from the coffee shop across the road.

The guy stopping for a break from jogging and checking his smart watch, his grin revealing his pride about his sport performance.

The young lad in a driving school car at the other side of the carpark learning to reverse and managing it perfectly at the third attempt.

The older lady looking carefully at the outdoor plant stall and selecting the two hanging baskets that will give her the most joy over spring and summer.

I stay where I am and repeat the 5-4-3-2-1 technique until driving finally feels safe. But before turning the engine on, I take a photo of the driving school car and add it to the folder on my phone. Others' happiness can revive mine.

Now, I am home. My eyes expelled their surplus tears; till the vessel is full again, they should stay dry.

I turn the key in the front door's lock.

I breathe in and I breathe out.

I take my trainers off.

I put them away.

I breathe in and I breathe out.

I take my coat off.

I put it away.

I breathe in and I breathe out.

I.

am.

exhausted.

Standing in front of the kitchen sink window, I look at the garden and observe the birds for a while. They are poking their beaks into the grass to catch worms. They fly away and rest on the fence panels before going back for more. I envy their lightness and their easy conquest of the space above, under and around them.

I breathe in and I breathe out.

Gently and purposefully.

I aim to attain serenity. No one could ever guess how much effort this requires, nor how hard I must work for happiness. It seems to come so naturally to other people.

The *Little Ball of Sadness* is back to being a *little* ball. I can resume my ten steps routine.

Today, I can do this. I can prevail. So, as the birds sing for me their light of hope, I tackle step 5. I put my apron on and start the washing up.

PIG 108239

BY TAYLOR MCLEOD

The chips had been hailed as a breakthrough for animal welfare. The chips would remove any negative feelings that an animal had and therefore, remove any allegation that the animals' needs were not being met. The chips would inform handlers what the animal needed at any given moment, be it food, water, movement or time outside, and so long as these were being met in a timely fashion - the general government guidance gave a time period of between 1-3 hours to address the needs of an individual animal - then there could not be any concerns raised about whether or not the animal's welfare was being protected.

As a byproduct of the chips, new jobs were also created. Veterinarians were soon encouraged to move into more tech focused roles, where they could use their deep understanding of animal biology to enhance the chips and to create newer versions that benefitted not only animals' welfare, but the job efficiency of animal handlers across the country. University courses soon started to offer new electives that would allow aspiring veterinarians to dabble in software engineering, and universities became a loud pioneer of how technology could be used to better animal welfare and provide humane alternatives to the long-standing traditions of factory farming.

The chips were initially rolled out over a period of two years and in those two years animal agriculture was seen to be revolutionised. Over the years that followed, the technology leapt from strength to strength to strength, and with every new cohort of inspired new veterinarians that entered the field, new innovations were made until the chips were marvelled at as a modern day miracle of scientific advancement. Yet technology is still only technology, and no matter how good a piece of software is, it only takes one small glitch to destabilize an entire software system.

There is an argument to be had as to whether or not this breakdown could have been avoided. Perhaps the night security guard could have noticed the flashing light on his screen, but he was too busy studying for his university course that he did not notice this. Perhaps the software engineer who was on call that night could have noticed that the chip server had gone down, but he was unfortunately dealing with another server breakdown for a banking system, so naturally that had to take priority. By the time he had fixed that problem, the chip server had rebooted itself and the system was back as it had been before. Perhaps if the manufacturing company that built the chip cared more about their product than their profits, they would have invested in a better server system that was not prone to overheating, and they likely would have hired more staff to run the routine checks on the server to ensure that it was running as intended.

But the server overheated and the server did what it had been programmed to do. It restarted itself. The server was still very high-tech and very much a state of the art piece of technology, but it was not magic and therefore even a fast reboot still took about fifteen minutes. Fifteen minutes may not seem like a lot of time to most people, but for the animals controlled by these chips, those fifteen minutes were a living nightmare. In most cases, the chips reset as soon as the server had rebooted, but for a small handful of animals, those fifteen minutes had been enough time to wake them up to their reality, and no matter how many times the chip tried to reset, there were certain thoughts that would never be silent again.

Pig 108239 was awoken from her sleep by an odd new sensation that she had not felt before. She tried to stand, but her legs felt numb, as if she had been lying on them for too long. She opened her eyes to see that it was still night, but there was an odd buzzing happening in her head. She tried to look around her but noticed that she was stuck in some sort of contraption that enclosed her. She could stand, but there was no way she could move around.

She slowly got to her feet, her body feeling alarmingly heavy and sore as she did so. Once upright, she noticed that the contraption she was in was smaller than she had thought, and due to her size she could feel the bars of the crate pressing against her swollen belly.

Her swollen belly? The buzzing in her head was slowly clearing and Pig could feel the precious life that was growing inside her. For a moment she had forgotten that she was due to have a litter of piglets very soon. She'd had many litters before, but this seemed to be the first time she was truly registering that she was going to actually have a litter. That piglets would come from her body and she would raise them.

But then, if this had happened before…where were her other piglets? She tried to recall what had happened to her last litter, let alone all the ones that came before, but she had no idea. She called out in desperation, a small part of her hoping that in the darkness, a cry she recognised would call back to her. But there was nothing other than the faint sound of other pigs beginning to move in the darkness around her, and they were all sounding just as confused as she was.

Then the darkness vanished and the lights came on above her. She was not sure what she had expected to see, but the sight of the dilapidated and filthy warehouse scared her. It felt familiar, but she could not recognise anything that she saw. The crate she was in held her fast to the one spot, although all she wanted to do was shrink away from the bright lights ahead of her and the long spider webs that were floating down from the ceiling above her. She looked down at her hooves to see that she was on a dirty, cold, concrete floor and suddenly the whole room seemed to be growing smaller.

She wanted to run. To escape. She didn't know

where she was but it all felt wrong. There was a strong stench of fear in the air as it seemed that every other pig around her was also coming to this new realisation. She did not recognise the warehouse, but she knew she had been here many times before. What had happened? This wasn't the home she knew, and yet something deep in her mind was telling her that she had always lived here. This wasn't the home she wanted. This was not the place she wanted to spend time in. Not a place that she wanted to raise her babies in. Yet she knew that this was the place that they would all die in.

Her screams mingled with the screams of the other pigs in the warehouse with her. They all tried to thrash against the sides of the crates that held them in their locked position, but all they did was injure themselves. Pig did not notice the aches on her body as the fear that was coursing through her body was powerful enough to dull every one of her senses. She screamed for her babies, for her freedom, for her body to stop aching, and for these horrifying moments to end. Yet her screams only mixed in with the screams of the other pigs, until all she could hear was their one collective plea for answers.

Their screams were suddenly cut off when Pig felt a painful jolt go through her head, as if a wasp had stung her somewhere deep behind her eyes. Yet it also made every other pig in the warehouse fall silent again, and when the buzzing stopped in her mind, Pig could only hear the content rustlings of the others in their pens, as if nothing had happened. The buzzing in her mind had been enough to distract her from the fear she had felt, and the sudden silence was deafening. She let out one more feeble cry for help, but no other pig joined her. A few snorted at the startling sound of her cry, but they quickly moved on. Again, as if she hadn't made a sound at all.

Pig felt her piglets move inside her. She had to get out of here. She had to get her babies out of here. Whilst she made no more noise for the remainder of the long night, she screamed her resolve loudly into her head so that she would not forget this horrible feeling.

"Freedom."

The message flashed across the screen. Tabitha looked at the screen and blinked a few times, confused by the word that was now slowly scrolling across the screen.

"That's odd." She muttered to herself.

"What is?" Jeremy said nonchalantly from his own screen, titling his head slightly towards her.

"This." Tabitha twisted her screen slightly so he

could easily see it and pointed with her finger at the word.

"Huh," Jeremy furrowed his brow as he looked at the word himself. "That is weird."

"I know, right?" Tabitha turned her screen back so it was directly in front of her as normal. "Is yours showing the same?"

"Which number is it?"

"Pig 108239."

"Huh," Jeremy muttered again as he clicked a few buttons on his keyboard and brought up the AI monitoring screen for the pig in question. "Yeah I can see it on my screen too."

"It has to be a glitch right?"

"Of the chip or the system?"

"Well…either?"

"I've never known of the system to glitch at all but I guess the chip is more prone to it."

"Have you ever seen a chip glitch?"

"No," Jeremy said with a sigh. "But logically speaking it has probably happened before."

"Shall we ask Manon?"

"You can do." Jeremy shrugged his shoulders. "No idea where she is, though."

"I might go and speak to her." Tabitha said as she disconnected her tablet from the main monitor and stood up from her desk. "Wait for me and then we can go do the rounds?"

"Sure thing." Jeremy said, his attention now back on his own screen as he went back to whatever report he had been working on before.

Tabitha left the office space and headed down the corridor to the large co-working space in the middle of the floor. She found Manon sitting in one of the private working booths with her noise-cancelling headphones on, no doubt trying to get through the very indepth welfare reports that the other veterinary clinicians had sent to her for final approval.

"Manon?" Tabitha knocked on the side of the booth as she spoke, hoping not to scare Manon from her thoughts. Manon looked up at her and for a brief moment seemed to struggle to place who she was and why she was in front of Manon. Then her face softened and she gave her a tired smile as she pulled the headphones off of her ears.

"Everything alright?" Manon asked and gestured to the other side of the booth for Tabitha to sit down.

"Very quick thing," Tabitha said as she sat down and unlocked her tablet. "I was doing my initial monitoring checks before Jeremy and I go do the rounds, and noticed this," Tabitha held up the dashboard for Pig 108239 and pointed again at the word.

"Huh," Manon furrowed her brow. "That is odd."

"I think it may just be a glitch, but have you ever come across this before?"

"I have seen glitches happen in the chips - is this on any of the other animals?"

"No, just this one."

"So it can't be the system. Must just be the chip acting up."

"What do you do with a faulty chip?"

"Technically it is for an engineer to fix. I don't think there is a way for us to reset the chip ourselves." Manon sat back against the high back of the booth and folded her arms across her chest, a move she always did when she was deep in thought. "You haven't done your rounds yet?"

"No, not yet. I wanted to talk with you first to see if we should fix the issue first before we head off."

"Head off. Check to make sure the pig hasn't knocked their head or anything that could have caused the chip to glitch. Then we can go from there." Manon said with a firm nod to Tabitha, who nodded back with a smile.

"Sure thing. Are you coming for these rounds?" Tabitha asked as she exited the booth.

"Not today." Manon said with a sigh. "These bloody reports will likely take me all day to read and if I just get them done, I can then stop having night-mares about them."

"We'll be there for about an hour if you need a break." Tabitha said reassuringly and then she headed back to the office to find Jeremy, who she found playing on his phone in the largely deserted office.

"Ready?" Tabitha asked as she entered. Jeremy nodded and the two of them left the office together and made their way to the elevator to head down to the barns where the farm animals were kept.

"What did she say?" Jeremy asked as the lift quietly dropped them down the six floors to ground level.

"Manually check on the pig first and then if the issue is still showing we can phone the engineers." Tabitha reported back with a shrug.

"Ah the sweet life of an engineer." Jeremy said with a wistful look in his eyes.

"What do you mean?"

"Well the engineers have the best part of the job, don't they? They get to sit in very nice office set ups and just play with the tech code, whilst we vet techs have to actually deal with the animals."

"Why is the engineers' job better?" Tabitha asked, genuinely confused as to what point Jeremy was trying to make.

"We're a bit unnecessary don't you think?" Jeremy said simply.

"Oh not this again." Tabitha rolled her eyes.

"I'm just saying, if the chips tell us how the animals are, why do we need to be here?"

"I'm not having this conversation with you again." Tabitha said dismissively, but then she felt bad when she saw how defeated Jeremy suddenly looked. "Are you still thinking about switching to the engineer route?"

"I dunno." Jeremy said with a small shake of his head. "Yes? No? Ask me again in an hour and I'll have changed my mind again."

"I think if you have to question it this much, you know what the answer should be." Tabitha tried to say gently, but Jeremy gave a small huff which suggested that the sentence had come out a little bit more blunt than she had intended. "Sorry, I didn't mean that to-"

"No, no, you're fine." Jeremy said with a small smile to her. "Just I know you're right. My parents keep saying the same thing to me but I just can't seem to take the plunge. Either one feels like a mistake, you know?"

"I know." Tabitha lied. She didn't know. She had no idea why Jeremy had such a hard time choosing, especially since as far as she was concerned he had already made his choice when he chose to go the vet tech career route and not the engineering route. If he wanted to switch it would likely cost more money and time to retrain, although at least with the vet tech background he wouldn't be starting completely from scratch. But still, vet school had nearly killed Tabitha with the intensity of the training. The thought of having to go near any sort of educational system still seemed like a fate worse than death in her eyes. The only way she would ever go back to education was if someone else paid for her to do it, and even then it would have to come with so many benefits that it would likely bankrupt the organisation willing to pay for it all.

The elevator doors opened silently and the two colleagues made their way across the bright office building and out into the small courtyard that sepa-rated the office part of the facility to the animal side of the facility. They neared the closest warehouse building and swiped their ID badges through the security doors so that they could enter where the animals were kept.

The animals were kept in large, open pens within the barns, separated by species and, if needed, by sex. The barn seemed very quiet today, although the occasional snort from a pig or gentle moo from a cow could be heard echoing around the building. Around each pen were large pathways that would be used to transport the animals in and out of the pens as needed, but also acted as walkways for the veterinary staff to inspect and monitor the animals without needing to actually enter the pens. Whilst the animals were of no threat to the humans who watched over them, rare instances had meant that these procedures were needed just in case of the worst case scenario.

Tabitha and Jeremy walked along the paths, waving and nodding to the few other vet techs that were also doing their own rounds at the same time. Various animals were kept in these barns, but as she was a porcine specialist she didn't get to spend much time with the other pens and the different animals that existed within them. Although she found them all fascinating, and tried to do her rounds ever so slightly slower than she should so she could spend more time just watching the animals go about their day.

"That's odd." A bovine vet tech was staring at their tablet with a confused look on his face just as Tabitha and Jeremy walked past.

"Everything alright Alfie?" Jeremy asked.

"Dunno..." Alfie responded, more to himself rather than to Jeremy's question. "I've been getting some weird readings today."

"Weird how?" Tabitha asked as she and Jeremy shared a knowing glance with one another.

"Like this," Alfie said and he showed them both the tablet screen. It looked identical to the dashboards they had for the pigs, except Alfie's had an image of a cow and was listing various different bovine traits that needed to be monitored. There was a small box at the bottom of the dashboard that showed what the animal was thinking about most, which was usually food or water or sunshine, but in this box it simply said 'calves'. "That's odd right? I've never seen that before."

"Has she just had a calf?" Jeremy asked, looking into the pen which currently appeared to house twelve large cows. They were mostly chewing on hay and grass, their tails swishing to in a calm and relaxed manner. Except for one cow in the back, who was staring straight ahead at the double doors that lead out into the open pasture.

"Is it her?" Tabitha asked, gesturing with her head towards the cow in the back.

"Yeah," Alfie said, his head now tilted slightly to one side as he watched the cow for himself. "She had a calf a couple days ago, and this message has shown each day. But this is the first day it's been there for more than a few minutes."

"So she's thinking about her calf?" Tabitha asked.

"The chips shouldn't let her do that." Jeremy said, a tiny pang of panic in his voice.

"Must just be a glitch right?" Alfie said as he now looked at Tabitha and Jeremy. "Right?"

Tabitha and Jeremy looked at each other for a moment.

"Well actually-"

Pig 108239 was back in the familiar farrowing crate, but what had once brought her comfort now brought her a feeling of deep apprehension in her stomach. Her tiny piglets had all been delivered safely, but as it was now her eleventh litter, she knew what needed to be done in order to ensure that her children were all safely born. Their tiny little bodies looked so weak and feeble compared to her, and she looked tiny compared to the lumbering farmers that routinely walked past her in this warehouse.

She had tried to ignore the visions of her last litter, but the sound of piglet thumping echoed around her mind as she tried to sleep. Even in the noise of the general population warehouses, she could only hear that deep, echoing thud as her piglet's head had collided with the wall. She had hoped it was only a nightmare, but this time she had seen it happen again. Not to one of her piglets but to various different piglets that had arrived earlier than her litter had. She had watched as the handlers picked up the wiggling bodies of the piglets and proceeded to walk so calmly towards the side of the warehouse. The thud would echo around the warehouse and yet only she appeared to react to it. She had tried to call out to the other pigs, but they all just stared at her blankly or snorted their disbelief at her. The handlers had seen her reacting and had approached her with their little black box, and whilst she felt a little shock go through her head, it did nothing to calm her down. If anything it only made her more angry. As if these humans truly thought they could silence her.

A few days ago, whilst she waited for her litter to arrive, she had cried out to the handler to stop him carrying yet another piglet to that dreaded wall. He had looked down at her and used his little black box. She felt the buzz briefly in her head, but she would not be quiet. She would no longer be silent with this. She cried out to him, angry now that he was trying to ignore her, and his response was to strike her hard on her head with the black box. The force of his hit rippled all along her body and Pig realised that she was meant to stay quiet. The pigs around her were quiet because they were made to be so, and if the little black box and the buzzing didn't achieve that, then these humans would resort to whatever tactics worked the best.

She would now stay silent, but if anyone tried to take her piglets from her, she would kill them. Or in the very least, severely maim.

The farmer walked towards her pen. She watched him lean over the side of the pen and saw his hands reaching towards her newest litter, their tiny pink bodies barely used to their own legs as they hobbled clumsily around, completely oblivious to their new surroundings. Pig's own legs felt heavy beneath her but she forced herself to stand as quickly as they would allow. In doing so, she shook the farrowing crate and this caused the farmer to stop and jerk his hand back, clearly spooked. Which is what she had wanted. Not this time. Not this litter. She couldn't turn her body at all to face him head on but from the corner of her eye she could see him once again reaching over the side of the pen, his horridly long fingers inching closer to one of her new sons. She kicked out with her back leg, her hoof hitting the end of the crate and sending a loud clattering noise around the warehouse that they were trapped in. The farmer shot backwards again and swore under his breath.

The farmer moved to stand directly in front of her at this point. Pig gave a small huff and her babies all obediently moved into the safety of the sleeping box at the back of the pen so that they would be hidden from sight. The farmer approached and reached out a hand to grab one of the babies as they hurried past Pig to get to the cubby hole. She threw herself as hard as she could against the side of the farrowing crate, rocking on her feet to cause as much noise as possible. Again the farmer swore under his breath, clearly distressed by the sheer power that Pig was exhibiting. He had never seen this in any animal before, and his ignorance of natural animal behaviour showed in the frustrated and confused look on his face. He reached towards Pig this time, waving his hands in her face as if attempting to scare her or disorientate her, but Pig had seen this trick before with the other handlers. It wouldn't work. She instead focused on the face of the farmer and lunged towards his outstretched hand. His fingers were just close enough to the crate that her snout was able to slip through the gaps and she caught his stupidly long fingers in her mouth.

His face contorted in agony as his free hand lashed about but it only connected with the outside of the crate, no doubt making his pain worse. Maybe there was a benefit to this crate, Pig thought to herself as she clamped down harder with her teeth, feeling the bones in his fingers breaking, the warm taste of his blood in her mouth. The more he struggled, the worse the injury was becoming, but it seemed the handler had not yet worked that out and his panicked screams were soon ricochetting off the dull warehouse walls. He struggled against her for a moment longer and then with one agonising tug, he pulled his hand back from Pig's mouth, but left two of his fingers behind.

She stared at him as he scrambled away from her pen, tripping over his own legs as he stared, horrified, at his mangled hand.

Good luck grabbing at my babies now, Pig thought as she let the fingers fall to the floor.

Tabitha walked through the pigs in their farrowing crates, checking the screens in front of each pen to ensure that all of them were getting what they needed. She was still unsure about whether she agreed with the continued use of the farrowing crates, but had to remind herself that the pigs could ask to leave them if they wanted, and so far none had done so. She loved seeing the new piglets each new cycle, with their tiny curly tails and their little squishy bodies that looked so pink and clean. She could happily sit in this warehouse all day and watch the piglets run back and forth in their pens, making sweet little oinking noises the whole time. Piglet litters were always her favourite, although she always tried to see the chicks hatch as often as she could in between her usual duties.

Somewhere in the distance, a deep howling scream echoed on the wind. Tabitha stood upright, as did the other people in the warehouse with her.

"Did you hear that?" Tabitha asked Jeremy, who had stopped tinkering with one of the information screens on one of the pens to look in the direction the scream had come from.

"Was that human?" he asked, his face one of confusion and apprehension.

"Shit -" exclaimed one of the farmers, who dropped the broom he had been using onto the ground with a loud crash and began searching his pockets for his radio.

"Is everything alright?" Jeremy asked tentatively.

"Ah fuck, man-" The farmer fumbled with his ear piece. "Can you repeat that Pat? What do you mean, bit him? His hand? What do you mean his fucking hand's gone? Fuck-" The farmer made a hurried exit from the warehouse, leaving the door to swing back and forth as he was in too much of a rush to stop and close it.

"His hand's gone?" Jeremy repeated, his face looking a little white as he turned to look at Tabitha, as if she would have any more idea of what was happening.

"Come on, we should follow," Tabitha said and she headed for the door, Jeremy right behind her.

They followed the now assembling crowd to outside one of the other warehouses. As they approached the growing crowd, they could hear the whispers as the story of what had happened slowly made its way from the inner circle to the newcomers on the outside.

"It bit his hand off!"

"I heard it only took a few fingers."

"A few fingers? I saw the wrist bone!"

"I bet he'll get a nice pay out though once the union hears of this."

Tabitha pushed her way forward and as people saw her approaching, they luckily began to clear a path for her to get to the injured person quicker. That was one of the perks of being a veterinarian, as everyone believed she could deal in the first instance with any sort of injury that took place. Despite the improvements in tech and welfare, staff injuries were still a surprisingly common occurrence.

Just outside of the warehouse door, a man was sitting on the floor, his right arm held high above his head in an attempt to stop the considerable wound from bleeding too heavily. Tabitha quickly looked at the injury and whilst the blood made it hard to see the real damage, the man definitely still had his hand, albeit he was clearly missing two of his fingers.

"It bloody bit me." He was muttering.

"Have you called an ambulance?" Tabitha said as she knelt down to look at the man. He was sweaty and deathly pale, and was very clearly on the brink of shock and passing out. She was pleased that a makeshift tourniquet had been placed on his arm and someone else was in the process of wrapping a shirt around the injured hand to stop some of the bleeding.

"It's been called. Should be in here in ten." One of the veterinary nurses in the bovine department said as she rummaged in her own supply bag for some bandages.

"Have you found the fingers?" Tabitha asked and the farmers in the area all looked at her in horror. "If she hasn't eaten them then the doctors might be able to reattach them."

"I think I'm going to be sick-" One farmer said and he turned away from the scene with his hand over his mouth. Tabitha winced slightly and gave the vet nurse a signal to say that she was going to go look in the warehouse. She didn't want to say anything more in case more people became queasy at her comments. She sometimes forgot that handlers were not medically trained, and so talk of blood and guts was not a normal topic of conversation the way it was for veterinary staff.

The warehouse was oddly quiet, but then that was what the chips were designed to do. The other pigs seemed completely oblivious to anything that had happened and they all seemed to be at peace in their pens. The only noise came from the pig in question, who was screaming in anger and thrashing her body against the sides of her farrowing crate. Tabitha approached and saw that the piglets had all retreated to their separate sleeping area at the back of the pen, so were all safe from the pig's stomping hooves and powerful pushes against the crate that confined her. This was the first time Tabitha had ever seen a pig in this state and it sent a horrible shiver down her spine.

She drew nearer and searched the bottom of the pen for sight of the man's fingers. There were drops of blood all over the floor and all over the pig's mouth, however she could not see the fingers. She debated entering the pen to look for them, but the pig was rocking side to side, suggesting that she was ready to attack anyone who came near to her. She tapped the screen at the front of the pen and tapped the small icon that was usually used to check on the status of the chip and the animals' needs. Except the message currently showing sent an icy chill throughout her body.

"DO NOT TOUCH MY BABIES."

Pig 108239 had been standing guard for four days now. Her body ached and she wanted to lie down, but if she lay down then her babies would not be able to hide underneath her. She watched the faces of the different humans who walked past her, all of them with faces of anger and fear as they stared at her. She made sure to stare straight back at them. Unblinking. Unwavering. They would not touch her babies again.

She had tried to warn the other pigs around her, but whatever that little black box did to them meant none of them listened to her. She had tried for two days to make them hear her cries of anger and panic as the farmers continued to abuse their piglets, but one little click on the black box and the other pigs all went silent again. Just when she thought she might have been getting through to some of them, their faces would go from confused to blank and they would go back to their blissful ignorance.

But at least her babies were safe. She would ensure that at least her babies would not be hurt again. Part of her wished that she could ignore it. A part of her longed for that joyful and easy feeling that came with not knowing reality. But she did know. She had seen that farmer slam her tiny baby against a wall and that was an image that played in her mind every day. She could still hear the thudding echoes that had rippled across the warehouse when her baby's head had hit that solid wall. Those nightmares were enough to keep her mind wide awake, and no matter what the farmers tried to do to her, and no matter what those odd farmers in the white coats tried to do to her, she was not going to forget the sight and sound of her dying baby.

Guilt gnawed at her. How many times has that happened? This was her eleventh litter. She must have had over a hundred babies. How many of them had met a similar fate? How many of them had she seen die and not even realise? The anger she felt seemed to boil her from the inside. She wanted another farmer to come along and try to take one of her babies again. The last one lost fingers but next time she did not plan to let go.

The farmers could see that in her eyes. She wanted them to see it. She got a small jolt of joy whenever she saw a farmer walk past her and wince at her searing glare, or saw how they jumped into the air if she made the slightest movement as they walked past her pen. Whenever a farmer walked past she called her babies towards her and they huddled obediently underneath her, her fat and stocky body sheltering them from any of the outside world.

A new farmer approached as Pig stood there. This one was in one of the strange white coverings that seemed to identify to the other farmers that this one was not one of them. This one however did not look scared when she approached Pig's pen. This one went to the screen that was in front of each pen and let out a heavy sigh.

"I'm going to get you out." The special farmer said quietly. She leant forward, and whilst Pig braced herself, she did not feel a threat from this one. Perhaps it was the sadness in her eyes, or the way she spoke, but Pig watched her carefully as she leant over the side of the pen and reached out a dainty hand towards her.

"I will get you out of here. Either the right way or the wrong way. Whatever way that may be." The special farmer was speaking more to herself than to Pig, but Pig let her. Her hand was gently outstretched, reaching towards Pig. Pig stayed still as the special farmer placed her hand on the top of Pig's head, in between her ears, and gently rubbed her hand back and forth across the top. It was an odd feeling that no farmer had ever done to her before, but Pig did not dislike it. It felt calming, and Pig let her body relax slightly, for the first time in four days.

"I will save you and your babies." The special farmer gave a soft smile, and Pig saw the glint in her eyes as the determination made her voice strong and forceful. Maybe she meant her words. Maybe she didn't. For now, Pig decided to trust her just enough to allow the head rubs to continue. Maybe when Pig did break herself and her babies out of this terror, she would not harm this special farmer.

The other farmers, however, Pig fully intended to punish.

The meeting room was filled with fancy and important looking people in suits that were all related to the farming industry in some way; Most were shareholders of various different farming companies, with a few journalists or marketing staff sprinkled into the mix. They listened to Tabitha's speech as though watching a child's nursery nativity play: painfully dull, yet hilariously entertaining at the same time with how silly the whole thing was. Tabitha knew she had lost them as soon as she told them about the situation with Pig 108239, but she had hoped she could have convinced them with the evidence, the other animals that had shown the same behaviour on other farms, and they would change their minds and actually take her recommendations on board. Manon stood to the side, shooting Tabitha encouraging looks throughout the presentation and giving her a reassuring look once she had finished. She had done all she could do but somehow Tabitha knew it wasn't going to be enough. She had spent the last few weeks preparing the data, the evidence, and the possible solutions, and she had barely slept last night for fear that even that still wouldn't be enough. As she finished her talk, and clicked on the last slide which showed the department's generic contact details, she realised with an angry and sinking heart that all of it really had not been enough.

"So…the pig wants out?" A woman in a suit to the left of the room said, her face further adding that this entire meeting could have been an email in her opinion.

"Yes, but-" Tabitha began.

"So let it out?" The woman responded simply, her face once again adding the silent 'duh?' that was meant to follow her statement.

"It is not so much wanting out of the barn." Tabitha repeated part of her presentation again. "Pig 108239 wants out of the system entirely."

"The system? So…the barn?" A man on the right of the room now chimed in.

"No," Tabitha took a short breath in. It was becoming painfully obvious now that not a single one of these shareholders had actually paid any attention to her presentation. "She wants out of the agriculture industry. She wants her freedom."

"To do what with?" Another voice called out but Tabitha could not see who had actually spoken.

"Whatever she wants." Tabitha couldn't help but shrug her shoulders at this comment. "What would you do if you had freedom?" There were a few murmurs throughout the room as people discussed the question with their neighbours, but no one gave an actual answer.

"But it is more than just Pig 108239." Tabitha went back through her presentation and brought back up the graph again. "A number of animals have seemingly overridden the welfare chip and are demanding their freedom back. This is not isolated to one chip, or one farm's server. It is a clear flaw in the hardware itself."

"Can't we just reset their chips?" A woman asked.

"We did. Multiple times." Tabitha tried to keep her voice calm. "And each time, these same animals have overridden their chips and are now asking for their freedom."

"What happened the first time?" Someone in the crowd asked.

"The first time what?" Tabitha asked.

"The first time you noticed this, what had happened?"

"The chip servers malfunctioned and all the welfare chips across the country stopped working for about fifteen minutes. It happened over night, and was labelled as a glitch on the tech side. But it seems in those moments, some of the animals became aware of their situation and even when the chips came back online and were working normally again, the animals remembered that moment of clarity."

"Make better chips?"

"Are you serious?" Tabitha spoke before she could think about the words, and a little disapproving ripple went through the crowd. "As in, are you actually suggesting that new welfare chips be produced? Or was that rhetorical?"

"Well you're a welfare officer, so you can't really speak on this." Another nameless voice spoke out. Tabitha noted the slight hostility in their voice.

"No, I can't." Tabitha agreed. "But from a welfare perspective, I don't think changing the chip will change the situation. Plus I don't need to be an engineer to know that new chips would take months, if not years, to be produced. And then who knows how many years more until they can be rolled out as replacements across the country. "

"But if we make the chips stronger, the animals can't speak out against them."

"But they already have. We have already heard what they wanted. Adding in stronger chips won't change that."

"Yeah but we won't have to hear about it again."

There it was. There was the reality of it all. Jeremy had told her this would be the response but Tabitha had been sure that this would not be the outcome. She had been so sure of her presentation, so trusting in the evidence that she'd been convinced the corporate higher ups could not ignore it. But they had. Because they didn't like it. They didn't like what they saw so they were seeking to find a solution that would hide all of that evidence from them. Jeremy could be a bit of a conspiracy nut at times and his pessimistic outlook could be draining, but Tabitha felt a wave of sadness wash over her that he was actually correct. Everything she had done, all of the proof she had placed before them, and Jeremy had still been right. Even sadder though was that she knew Jeremy would probably be upset that he was right about something like this for once.

"I'm sorry?" Tabitha asked simply. "Not sure I follow." She did, but she needed to hear it again from them.

"Well if we make a stronger chip that they can't

'override'-" The man now speaking made little quotation marks at this word with his fingers. "Then we can go back to farming them as normal and their welfare is still very much intact."

"But-" Tabitha began but she caught Manon's eye and saw the defeated look on her face. This was not the time and this was definitely not the place to be having this conversation on repeat. None of the people in this room wanted to have the conversation to begin with and there would be nothing to gain by continuing to push the subject. 'No more juice from that squeeze', as Tabitha's mom would have said. She gave Manon a small nod and Tabitha saw her switch to her corporate persona in an instant.

"That's all from us today, and clearly lots to be discussed. Thank you all for your time today. If you have any questions at all, our department contact details are at the bottom of the hand out." Manon could command a room in a way that Tabitha had never seen, and with the pasted smile on her face Tabitha nearly missed the seething rage that burned behind Manon's eyes. Tabitha hoped she was hiding her emotions just as well, but she could already tell that if one person tried to speak to her as she returned to her seat then she would likely burst into tears. Or perhaps just punch someone. She wasn't sure which would be worse.

She retook her seat towards the back of the hall and Manon joined her shortly afterwards.

"We reassess." Manon whispered to her gently as the next department speaker stood up to give their presentation. "We will find a solution."

Tabitha gave Manon a reassuring smile and small nod of her head in agreement, but she already had a solution. She had been thinking of this solution since she first saw Pig 108239 ask for her freedom and it was the solution she had been fighting against in her mind ever since. She was still not convinced if it would help, but she had tried to do it the professional way and that had fallen on ignorant ears. So now she would try it the unprofessional way.

It was the first time she had felt some semblance of calm in weeks.

Tabitha and Jeremy looked at each other one last time.

"Will this work?" Tabitha said.

"It has to work." Jeremy responded with a sigh. "If it doesn't then I have to kiss both of my potential careers goodbye."

"It will go out to every single computer? Every device?"

"If it is connected to the internet, it will receive this."

"Do it."

"Are you sure?"

"Are you sure?"

"We haven't come this far to only come this far."

"For her?"

"For her."

Tabitha gripped Jeremy by the shoulders as he clicked around on the computer screen and entered the code into the system. He took a long, shuddery breath in and then clicked the initiation button. It all looked like a lot of insane ramblings to her, with numbers and symbols and odd words scattered throughout, but this was Jeremy's language and she needed to trust him.

Tabitha braced herself for something big to happen. She hadn't known what to expect but the silence was scary. She and Jeremy looked at each other for a moment, eyes trying to read one another to see if the other knew what was happening. Then her phone vibrated with an alert. And then her tablet. Then the computers around them beeped with notifications.

"You check first." Jeremy said to her, holding his own phone out as far as he could as it continued to vibrate with notifications, as if it was going to explode at any moment.

Tabitha unlocked her phone and saw the messages that were coming in.

> Bovine 33982: Where have my babies gone?

> Chicken 199209: My wings feel so heavy.

> Pig 30881: I can't move in this crate.

> Sheep 96648: These shaving wounds won't ever heal.

> Bovine calf 10478: Where's my mummy?

> Lamb 29011: Where did my sister go?

The messages came in a never ending stream. Message after message from the chips that were now deactivated and the animals were free to speak their minds for the first time in their lives. People would hear their pleas now whether they wanted to or not.

Across the country, a number of the farm shareholders were being woken up by their phones reading out all of the messages that they were receiving. What had once been a very useful hack for the shareholder to be able to read emails and messages without needing to actually open their phone themselves now seemed to scream at them with the voices of thousands of animals that they were legally responsible for. They would try to turn the setting off but still their phone would vibrate. If they tried to turn the phone off, and turn to their tablet or computer for more information on this weird scenario, the voices now moved here. Pop up after pop up, message after message, plea after plea, that these shareholders could no longer ignore and could not turn off.

In the main office. Manon watched the messages flash across her screen and across the screen of every other member of the company that was currently on site. They were calling out to one another in panic, wondering why the computers were suddenly seeming to turn against them and no amount of code was turning it off again. Manon took a small delight in playing along with it all. She did not know for certain, but her intuition told her what the cause of this was. She would never ask for the truth, as her having plausible deniability in all of this was likely key to the overall success of this stunt, but she gave a small smile as her mind immediately went to Tabitha, and no doubt Jeremy too, huddled away with some ancient version of a computer that could not be traced and cheering along with them as the messages sent the entire office into some sort of breakdown.

In the warehouse barns, the animals became restless and started to call out to one another. Pig 108239 looked around her at her companions and saw the confused fear in their eyes as they finally were awakened to the situation. Now was the time. She called her companions to her side and with their combined force they were able to break down the flimsy fences that had once seemed so formidable and strong to them. As they made their way to the main barn doors, the animals in the other pens saw what they were doing and copied them, with many of the animals being able to simply slip through the fences that had once caged them. The humans had never expected the animals to want to escape - they had made sure that the animals never wanted to escape - so they had made no effort to keep the pens secure. Basic materials and shoddy work meant the animals could easily break through. Now all that stood in their way was the barn door itself.

As Pig 108239 and her herd of animals approached the barn door, it opened just wide enough for a small group of humans to appear. They were terrified and unprepared, having no more than a few planks of wood to wield as some sort of protection. Why pay for protection when all aggression has been removed from an animal? Pig 108239 squealed and broke into a run straight for the barn door, the rest of her new herd following quickly behind her, their cries colliding together in a symphony of defiance. The humans all immediately jumped out of the way, and the few that did not move quick enough were simply tossed painfully to the side as the animals stampeded past them, past the other barns, and out into the wild open fields that lay before them. No fences, no pens, and no chip to limit what they could do anymore.

All across the country, as the humans grappled with their new moral landscape, the animals disappeared into their wild freedom.

SHOOTING STARS

BY CÉCILE KEEN

teach 28 *Little Stars*, aged seven and eight. They are young enough to retain the fresh curiosity of childhood and mature enough to understand that their future could follow an array of pathways, all different from each other and from what they have ever known so far.

In our school, each class has a symbol that assigns an identity, which is built upon year after year. The Kindergarten teacher develops resilience through positive attitude. Her *Little Happy Faces* graduate to *Little Owls*, as exploring for clues to answer questions is the Grade 1 class motto. Teaching is the most rewarding vocation, to which I have dedicated over 10 years. I wish for my happy clever little students to shine so bright that they can aim as high as the sky, wherever their ambitions take them. Thus, for my Grade 2 symbol, I chose *Little Stars*.

We live in a deprived area of Austin, Texas. One must not confuse deprived with neglected or unloved, quite the contrary. Deprived means a tough daily struggle for parents, who do their utmost to provide. But it also means the horizon line is often drawn very close to home, so forget about the pot of gold under the rainbow. All parents, whoever they are - them, you, my husband and I - limit their children's experience for three reasons: unfamiliarity, dislike and budget. The combination of all three is the situation for most of our families. It is up to our school to make up for it, but breaking such a powerful trio of boundaries is hard work.

In the usual lifestyle of our catchment area, children eat their supper watching *America's Got Talent* or similar reality shows, where participants are hailed for their talent but ridiculed for their imperfection. If having the guts to have a go leads to public mockery, how can our young generation recognise that failure only lies in not trying? How do we empower children to believe in themselves and to trust that anything is in their reach provided they give it a chance?

Therefore, in Grade 2, the children collect star stickers for suggesting an aspiring idea. That's how we mapped out the routes to become President of the United States.

"We can't be President!"

"Why ever not? You can all shoot for the stars, don't you let anyone say otherwise".

I dismissed the boring *"Star of the Week"* certificate. Instead, we reward the *"Ambitious Star"* and the *"I had a go Star"*.

When we studied the yearly Geminid meteor shower, the homework was to spot the shooting stars at night. The fabulous illustrations painted in class the next day will be on show above the whiteboard all year. Our favourite activity is the monthly imaginary trip for which we position the chairs as in the vehicle we would travel in. The excitement this simple idea generates is wonderful to watch. Next month, Apollo 11 will take us to the moon; we shall observe our solar system from the highest point of view mankind has ever reached.

Right now, we are not on one of our special trips. We are not boarding a fantasy plane, train or rocket. We are seated along the back wall of the classroom, where a fictitious Hollywood Walk of Fame has been made up with stars stuck down on the carpet. Each one bears a name. On a peg above, is hung a bag containing a personal comforter and lollypops.

No confusion where any of us must sit.

Doors locked.

Blinds down.

Lights off.

This is no practice. Practice was three weeks ago.

During the drill, everything worked perfectly: the metal detectors gave the first warning; the entrance's second set of double doors remained closed; the receptionist sent the red code alarm to all classrooms for teachers and students to get into position straight away and all doors locked automatically.

What failed us today?

When we heard gunshots followed by the thud of falling bodies in unimaginable shrieks of pain and fear, my *Little Stars* lost their glow to make themselves as invisible as possible. The instructions are clear: stay down in silence, and, above all else, do not move until help arrives.

Our building is not complicated: a long rectangle split by a corridor in the middle, reception at the front, classrooms on both sides, playground around in a U-shape. Each classroom has two doors, one inside, one outside. Since the intruder has passed reception, he can access every room, about 250 children plus 15 staff. Lucky are the ones who called in sick this morning because, today, our visitor is transforming the next safest place for children after their home into one of indescribable trauma. If we are fortunate to stay alive, this ordeal may well reshape my *Little Stars* into shadows of darkness. Will they fall into a black hole, or will they have sparks still left to light?

When the lockdown alarm rung, my initial instinct to run away needed smothering. One particular US President would arm teachers: more firearms, that's his best proposal to solve gun violence. With or without a weapon, my role has already shifted from educator to bodyguard. I am by the outside door, deemed the weakest point in the risk assessment. Of course, this implies the belief I could stop anyone from coming in. Today, this very spot might turn out to be the closest to safety; although there could be one or more other accomplices outside, for all I know. My car is in sight and perhaps I have a chance to escape: open the door, run through the playground to the parking lot, 15 seconds tops and I am free, safe to go home to my little boy. I could succeed if I take the risk, me, by myself, without children to slow me down or panic into chaos.

Caring is not the same as loving. I care deeply about my *Little Stars* and work tirelessly to help them reach their dreams, but I do not love them. I love my son, my awesome little one, who is recently out of diapers. He is my everything, the biggest star in my universe, the sun that lights my every day. I would die for him without a twinkle of a thought because I do not only care but love him. To protect the *Little Stars* in my class, does my boy have to lose his Mom? Amongst the parents, how many would make such a sacrifice for someone else's child? If none, why is it expected of me? Picture the papers' headlines: *"Coward Teacher abandoned 28 children to slaughter to save herself"*. I would most likely face being treated as a social pariah, like Joseph Ismay, the White Star Line chairman, who deserted the Titanic while women and children were still on board. The truth is, here or not, whatever will happen, will happen. I am 5'4" and 129 pounds. I am only a teacher. I attend weekly yoga classes, not combat training. I cannot save the children. But I will stay. The duty of care to my Little Stars includes the unspoken readiness to risk my life. Is it truly how far my duty will take me today?

Thunderous profanities are coming from the corridor spilling into our room, enveloping the children in a cold drape of unshakable terror. The banging on doors that remain closed leads to increasing frustration for the man, who releases his gun into the ceiling before reloading it. We are in the last room of the corridor and he's approaching. Somehow, he has gained entry into Grade 1, opposite us. Didn't the door lock properly? Ours did. Jenny, the class teacher, is talking with him. Her words cannot be clearly understood. She seems collected, speaking with a kind, soft and low voice. I may be mistaken but the way she talks makes me think she knows him. Since half of school shootings in the US are committed by former students, it is plausible our visitor has sat in my classroom too. If Jenny knows him, she may be able to reason with him. If she doesn't, her 35 years' experience and grand-mother look might calm him down and do the trick until the cops arrive.

But the man yells at her to be quiet. NO, he will NOT allow her to stay and let the children out. Who does she think she is to tell him what to do? He is the one in charge, no one else. He shouts he cannot think with that much talk, that his ears ache from her nonsense chatter, and he cannot stand anyone looking at him. He swears he needs a drink, whilst smashing items against the walls, presumably children's water bottles. "NOT THAT", he bawls.

And then all of a sudden, there is the sound of one single gunshot. I can no longer hear Jenny, but her voice might just be submerged by the children's cries. Is anyone hurt? Maybe the man has shot at the whiteboard, or maybe at the ceiling, or maybe at a desk, or at the library bookshelf, at the rainbow display, at the puppets' theatre, the animal alphabet, the painting corner, the maths area ... or the ... maybe ..., or ..., I don't know ..., the classroom is full of things, boxes, material, books, equipment, learning paraphernalia, that can be safely shot at. Or ... maybe ... someone is dead? But who? It could be Jenny, a few months away from her retirement. Her husband is her teenage sweetheart; if it's her, they will not live their golden years together. If it is a child, somebody will have to find the words to deliver the news to the parents.

The man is now howling about his head hurting like hell. He's fed up with the likes of them thinking they are better than him. He won't take it anymore and why should he? He's had enough! So, it has to stop. ENOUGH, do they know what ENOUGH means? Why can they not see it has to stop? And why can't they stop right now? In the same breath and at the top of his voice, he carries on throwing accusations: it is their fault, he has known all along what they've been up to. Don't they dare deny it. He hates them and they F**ING know why. They deserve what's coming. They must all shut up and quick. And look DOWN at the floor. They must LOOK DOWN at the BLOODY floor. If he catches anyone looking up or talking, that's it. Do they get it? It would be a bad, a very bad idea, oh yes, such a very bad idea to test him. So don't they even think of trying coz they will regret it, for sure. The eerie stillness that follows is long enough to fool us into hope, but that shatters when the erratic shooting starts and reverberates through the entire building. The man has come prepared. He has an assault weapon. It's one of those able to reel off 30 shots before it needs reloading, which takes hardly any time. Then it can fire another round of 30. And then another 30. And then another. And this goes on and on until the screams are entirely over. There is no uncertainty anymore: we know it is not a what, but a who he has shot at. The man has achieved exactly what he wanted: a forever mute and blind audience.

There may be something special about our school for this man to be here, and we may never know what that is. Either there is a link or the attack is random. Should there be no connection, out of the four schools in this area of town, the man happened to pick and walk into ours. We are at the wrong place at the wrong time, as they say. But we are not in the wrong. We are precisely where we should be, enjoying discovering and learning new things together. The only thing children have learnt today, is that the world is unsafe and they can be slain anywhere, even at school.

Where does this deranged need for shooting at children come from? What kind of a man plans and then performs such heinous crimes? There is no motive, illogically shaped or otherwise, that could absolve him. Whether his actions are grievance-filled or not, it makes no difference. The outcome is the same. The absence of conscience that allows him to shoot children at close range is too strong to comprehend. Yet I cannot believe there has not been at least one moment of lucidity from the time he bought the weapons to the time he physically made the first step out of his front door to embark on his mission. How long must this one moment of sanity last, for it to derail the evil madness of his undertaking? Isn't one split second enough?

This morning, while our children were having a hot chocolate and cereals for breakfast, chatting away or bickering with siblings, having their lunch pack made, waving "goodbye, see you later" to their Mom and Dad from the yellow school bus, our man was preparing his guns and ammunition.

Whereas many of my *Little Stars* are hugging their teddies, Nancy has pulled her bobble hat down, knees up, head in knees and arms around as if hugging herself. Tucker's bladder has let go; I throw him my sweater to sponge the liquid. Twins Hunter and Grayson are hiding behind their bulletproof backpacks that their mum bought thanks to additional cleaning shifts on Sundays. Aisha, who is next to me on my right, whispers so low that I nearly can't hear "Can you hold my hand, please miss? You won't leave us, will you?". "I promise you, I'm not going anywhere" I reply, in the same hardly audible voice. I put my arm around her shoulder to let her lean against me and keep her hands firmly into mine. Should someone watch us, they could not tell who is comforting who. Tamara, Ely and Dwight are paralysed with fear, eyes locked on our corridor door. If we get through this, their faces will haunt me for the rest of my time. In their mouths, children have one or two lollypops. It is part of the lockdown procedure. The sweet taste helps them keep quiet and calm. Gerald, our class clown, is sat crossed legged. He has eight lollypops, three in each cheek and two on his tongue, looking like a chipmunk. It is the sort of things he would do to make us laugh usually. His head is tilted to the right in order to hold his teddy bear between his chin and shoulder. His strong and solid grip with his two hands on the eight white sticks protruding out of his mouth betrays he is in no mood for comedy. The most lively and happy child of the class is completely still, with a vacant look, showing hardly any signs of breathing, in a state of petrification as if his gaze had met the Gorgon Medusa herself.

I'm shaking; coldness has little to do with it. I

should pray. But what do I pray for: for myself, for the children, for the whole situation to disappear or for my son to enjoy a happy life without me? Or I could make a pact with God. What can I offer Him in exchange for 28 lives plus mine?

My husband has not seen my text yet. Now or later, it does not matter. The Love of my life and our gorgeous little one will know they were with me to the end. Tomorrow or in a few days, my husband will find in our son's chest of drawers a newly bought tee-shirt, that I kept secret for a surprise this coming weekend. It will most likely happen in the morning, when he will dress our boy. He will look for a tee-shirt in the middle drawer on the left-hand side and, there, he will pick one he won't recognise, having never seen it before. He will unfold it, perhaps hold it up or put it flat on our son to check it fits. Then he will pay attention to the design and read the message printed on the front: *"Promoted to Big Brother"*. That's when his already shattered heart will break into a million more pieces than anyone could ever imagine possible, but there is nothing I can do to save him from the inevitable crushing despair that awaits him.

Now that the man has finished his job in grade 1, will he leave? Is he satisfied or hungry for more? There is no manual in Teachers' training to prepare for this level of horror. As the guidelines advise, we stay put and lay low, hoping the intruder will go somewhere else. How lame is that? Does it make me a bad person if I wish him to indeed go somewhere else, anywhere else, even in Grade 3, 4 or 5 ... as long as it is not Grade 2? My dishonourable bidding has no time to cause me shame because our man has simply crossed the corridor towards us.

He is now pushing down our door handle again and again, each time more furiously. He orders us to open the door and to open it NOW! The lack of response leads him to cackle that not to worry, he doesn't need our help, he will soon be in anyway. If we think we are clever, we better think again. He will show us in a minute or two how clever we're not. He doesn't like this blue door. His favourite color is red, haven't we guessed that already? By the time he's done, this STUPID door and everything else in this STUPID classroom, will be red, a lovely bright fresh red. He'll make sure of that. Don't we doubt it! With a vile snigger, he is kicking the door with greater determination. Between each kick, he's abusing us, without any restraint, in a verbal diarrhoea of repulsive insults. We are the rats of society, dirty things, the wretches of the earth, parasites, vermin to eliminate and so many more despicable names, which I refuse to hear, so I show the children to put their hands on their ears.

"Ready or not, here I come" he chants to an ominous tune, that he enjoys to the point of laughing, proud of his own revolting joke. I suddenly feel sick, turn quickly to my left to the outside door and manage to throw up screening myself behind my scarf, which I use to cover the vomit. I then sit on it to hide from the children what has happened and lessen the smell of my regurgitated morning coffee and bagel, as if that's of any importance in the current circumstances. Something sounds alarmingly different now. The man is like a wild beast attacking with unstoppable rage. He is using some sort of tool. The *"bangs"* and *"thuds"* are so loud and forceful … but what could it be? What has he brought with him? ……, a lump hammer, that's it, that's what he's got. Oh, may the Lord help us!

If we had the floor-to-ceiling bulletproof whiteboards teachers have been asking for the last four years, we would not be sitting here totally helpless. Within seconds of the lockdown, we would have turned the flat boards into a safe lockable bulletproof room. But Management denied our request each time because of budget restrictions. Bullet-proof desks were also discussed at length in the staff room.

They look like regular three-sides classroom desks. Students can scurry under, let the shield fall and conceal themselves inside. Our suggestion to the Headteacher met an unexpected response: "You can always buy your own, if you so wish. They cost about $9,000 a piece". Very few teachers could afford this. More to the point, no teacher would have one for themself but none for the children. How bitter tastes the remorse now! One desk could shelter Michelle and Harper, our two smallest children, probably Ron too actually. $3,000 a life seems like a good deal from my present viewpoint.

The School Managing Board may find some money in next year budget, if there are still children to teach of course. For now, here we are, down on the floor, waiting powerlessly for time to determine our fate. We are supposed to be quiet but are beyond that capability. In the absence of a safe room and safe desks, my crying *Little Stars* have gathered tightly around me. My arms are not big enough to embrace them all and magically create an eclipse that would obscure us into safety. They are stuck to each other, hugging, gripping any hand or arm available, holding on to human warmth.

They know what to expect. Despite barricading ourselves and pushing desks and chairs against the door to strengthen it, the only thing that separates life from death is really only that door and it will not hold much longer. A 2'6" by 6'6" piece of wood painted in bright sky blue: that is our only lifeguard, and it is about to break. A few more kicks, a few more thuds, and there shall be nothing, nothing left at all to stop this insane bloodthirsty monster from coming in.

In between the blinds on the windows, fleeting glimpses of cops can just be seen. All staff members wear a panic button that immediately notify the local police. Like me, my colleagues must have pressed their alert buttons because the policemen are here and have arrived quickly, not quickly enough for Grade 1 though. A few cops are running across the tarmac. Are they after other armed men outside or are they rushing to get in? With the police's shouting, the children's crying, the hammering attack on the door and the deafening vulgarities from the gunman, it is hard to think clearly, let alone make sense of what the cops are doing. If I knew for sure the schoolyard was safe, I would usher the children out, but there are no cops at the door to free us. There are no other children or teachers, that I can see, either. It must mean the playground is a no-go.

Could someone, anyone, please tell me what to do?

Which is best: hoping the door will hold on just a little bit longer or tempting our chance outside?

Please …

LIFE'S A STAGE
BY BERNADETTE LYNN

From outside, the building was rather boring; three or four stone stairs leading up to a double doorway set in a flat red brick wall darkened with years of petrol fumes. Metal bars over the windows demonstrated the run-down nature of the area and the faded sign over the door had needed repainting for several years.

Teri stood where the taxi had dropped her, marvelling at how shabby and unimportant it now looked, the life gone from it along with the play, although it had only ended last night. It had consumed her so recently yet was already in the past.

Inside was busy in a rather lacklustre way. Not many people were here to help with the breakdown of the set, only those who didn't have lives to get on with.

Weirdly, she didn't really recognise the set, though it was familiar in a deja-vu kind of way. It was a living room, a fake fireplace with yellow tissue paper lit up by a bulb and a nice, but battered, winged armchair she did recognise. This was the set for the last scene, that she'd barely been in, sitting in that armchair before the rest of the cast had come on for the finale. But this was the armchair from her living room, wasn't it? She'd fallen asleep in this armchair, last night, after the play, hadn't she? Only, when she thought about it, she didn't remember last night after the play at all. She'd been so tired when it was done: she didn't have the stamina of these young people. Of course, she'd lent the chair to the production. It had been her grandfather's, many decades ago, and was perfect for this set. She'd have to get someone to help her get it home later, it wouldn't be easy in a taxi.

"Morning," said Barney, irritatingly cheerful. "You look knackered, love. How's the head?"

"I'm shattered, but no hangover," she said. "Is there much left to do?"

"Plenty," he said. "It may have been a budget production this time but there's still a lot to clear. You really want that chair?"

"It's on its last legs, but it has sentimental value,"

she said. "It's been in my life as long as I remember. But it's a bit heavy to get home by myself."

Barney carried it off stage for her, and set it in the hall near the doors, nearly catching his trousers on the broken spring. The rest of the furniture was easier to clear. The small occasional table went into the space under the stage, the disintegrating rug straight into the bin, the fireplace dismantled and sorted into various boxes and shelves. The stage was bare now; that disquieting feeling of similarity to her own living room gone. She helped Barney and Chris take down the backdrop and roll it up.

"I'll be glad to paint over that, it was depressing," said Chris.

Teri started to say something about the view from the window and stopped, confused. There was a painted window, but with the curtains painted closed over it. She was thinking about her own window, which looked out over the valley and the farms and brought sunshine into the slightly dreary rented room. She was more tired than she'd realised, and it had been too long since she'd sat and looked at the view.

"All old people's living rooms are depressing," said Barney. "All souvenirs from places they'll never go again and birthday cards they never get rid of from people who never come and see them. Flotsam and jetsam left after the tide is out."

"That's a bit unfair," said Chris. "I just meant the brown; everything is brown and faded and that grotty old chair made it worse."

"Careful, Teri still has an attachment to that chair. She's going to resent that."

"It's OK," said Teri. "I know it's old and grotty. That's partly why I love it. For as long as I can remember, it's been part of my life. My Grandpa always sat in it after work, or when he came in from the garden. I'd sit on his lap and he'd read me stories. And then after he died, my father had it and did the same thing, though I was starting to get too big to sit on his lap by then. It's had a lot of use and heard a lot of stories, you can't blame it for being a bit worn out."

"That's how I'm feeling right now," said Chris. "Worn out and done with other people's stories. I'd love to do something really different, next time. Maybe go for a part myself."

"You could try asking. You've definitely served your time, backstage. Teri, love, could you move that curtain for us and we'll put this in the workshop?"

The curtain wasn't one she recognised either. Hanging from a square bar and, from this angle, hiding the wings, it reminded her of those in the hospital, last time she'd been an inpatient. The same kind of blue material, concertina-folded and light-weight. Had it been there for the play? Probably tied back out of the way, because apart from the memory of the hospital she didn't remember seeing anything like it, before.

Down in the workshop, there was a different feel. She always loved the smell here, of wood and varnish and paint. It reminded her of John's shed, where he'd retreated with broken toys or household items at weekends, emerging triumphant later with the repaired object.

Two people she didn't know well were busy at a carpentry bench: they were working on an old cot, splintery old beechwood like the one she'd had when her daughter was a baby. It even had a crack on the bottom bar. She'd cracked Sarah's by standing on it — only one foot, but she'd put too much weight on it while trying to clean up, that awful time when Sarah had simultaneously thrown up and leaked out of her nappy and Teri had had to clean the cot one-handed while holding a sick toddler who wouldn't be put down. John had been away, of course, a work thing — the children always got sick when he was away, or working late. Never when he was around to help.

Maybe that was Sarah's cot they were working on. Teri didn't remember what she'd done with it, when the children left home. Had John taken it to the dump, or a local charity shop? Those were exactly the kind of places where you'd source furniture for a play. Or maybe that bottom bar often broke on old cots, not designed to take a mother's weight. It was a nice memory though, now she had enough distance to laugh at it. Not nice at the time, but she missed those days when the children were small, when she was young and full of energy. They'd been so sweet, Sarah and Joe. Such good friends from babyhood, and things had been so much simpler when most problems could be fixed with a cuddle and a snack.

The cot was in pieces now, one of the men tidily collecting all the screws and sorting them into drawers, and the wave of nostalgic memory receded from Teri's mind as she watched. Now wasn't the time to indulge. She'd promised to help organise the props room.

There was another backdrop hanging on the stage as she walked past, but she left the men to do this one. It was a sunny, sandy beach, rather like the one they'd spent most of their holidays on, near the bungalow her aunt lived in. Teri had gone there every summer for a week, with her older sister, and both had carried on going down every year with their own children. Up until the tragedy, of course.

This scene had also had a dark edge, she

thought, though now she'd thought of her nephew that memory obliterated the show and the nicer thoughts she'd had, and she hurried on through the wings on the other side, through another hospital-style curtain, green this time, and into the hall. She wasn't going to think of Michael, or boats. It was one thing being in a nostalgic mood, another thinking about things she definitely wanted to leave in the past. But just the word 'past' triggered another memory: Michael, aged about five, sitting on his grandfather's knee in that grotty old winged armchair, six-year-old Joe on the other knee, while their Granddad told them about being in India during the war, and riding on an elephant. Both boys were fascinated and told Granddad with much excitement that they would both go to India and ride elephants.

Joe never had, though he'd ridden one in the zoo, back in the days before zoos decided that was cruel to the elephants. But Michael had spent three years after university teaching English somewhere in Asia and had sent home a picture of himself riding an elephant in the jungle somewhere. Teri's father had framed that picture and kept it on his mantlepiece until he died, and then Marjorie had taken it.

Barney would say that was depressing, she thought with a laugh, old people keeping their old photos, memories of a grandson who hadn't made it to thirty.

"Cheer up!" said Lizzie, sorting through the contents of a box marked 'kitchenware'. "Aren't you happy it's over? It was a hard run."

"I'm a bit nostalgic," said Teri. "Visiting memory lane. It's tiredness, mostly. You're right, it was a hard run. I barely remember what it was all about, there are so many scenes jumbled up in my head."

"I expect Mr Sinclair didn't help, messing everyone around at the last minute," said Lizzie. "What a jerk."

"Mr Sinclair?"

"You know, rich wanker who messed everyone around insisting that everything had to be done to his timetable?"

Teri didn't remember Mr Sinclair being at the play. She'd probably been busy backstage and missed the fuss. She was familiar with him, though. He was fairly young, about forty, with a much younger wife who he bullied: a wealthy local businessman and entrepreneur who'd run for the Council a few years back, and luckily — in Teri's eyes — failed. He'd raised objections to the revamp of the local Community Centre that had left all the Centre users in limbo for several years while the leaky roof got worse and the kitchen was closed off, all because the necessary building work would cause noise and dust and lorries up Red Lion Road where he lived, and he didn't want to be inconvenienced. The Lunch Club that Teri and so many other pensioners relied on for socialising had had to close. That was why the Amateur Dramatic Society had been such a lifeline for her recently, and it upset her to know that Mr Sinclair was causing trouble here too.

Many of the props that needed clearing away had once been Teri's. The carpet, which John had brought back from the Middle East after one of his business trips there and which had been the centrepiece of their living room for so many years. After the divorce, she'd had to get rid of it, because it wouldn't fit in the living room of her tiny new flat. Maybe it was a different, similar carpet: she couldn't remember the details any more, not after more than forty years. It was unlikely that it was the same one, she hadn't joined the group until couple of decades after that. Who had she given her carpet to? After all this time she didn't remember, but hers had been fraying at the corner in the same way — which is of course why she'd momentarily thought it was the same one. Then those big cushions — that unicorn one looked a lot newer, but was identical to Sarah's childhood favourite. Sarah had forgotten it when she grew up, and left home, but after the divorce Teri had put it in her bed, something to hug in those long, lonely nights when the new flat felt empty and she was so depressed.

Piles of unsorted props lay on the table, and Teri began to sort them out. They all seemed familiar, personal. What had these been used for, in the play? Surely no-one had carried an old Silver Jubilee mug on the stage? Or a set of war medals? Her grandfather had had a set just like this, serving in France in the First World War. He'd never spoken about it in her hearing; he'd been just twenty-four and had left his young wife and three-year-old son (Teri's father) to go and shoot at other young men from the trenches and even Dad had never heard him talk about it. They'd found the medals and a pile of letters he'd written to Granny in his top drawer after he'd died, some from that war and some from the Second World War. Teri and her sister had believed that Grandpa was a spy, because he'd refused to talk about what he did, but later she'd decided he found it too painful. Dad had talked more: not about fighting or the army, but about India where he'd served during the Second World War, about tigers and elephants and temples in the jungle. He'd also had medals from that time, and both had attended the local Remembrance Day service every year without fail right up until they died.

Here was a belt, embossed leather similar to the one Teri had given to John for his birthday, just after they got engaged. A silver-framed photo of a school class, Teri in the front row in her primary-school uniform, probably their final year at St Jude's. This didn't look like the copy Teri had on her mantlepiece at home, though the frame was the same: in this picture all the faces were as sharp as in her memory, only a little faded with age. A trophy — and this made her gasp aloud, so Lizzie looked over at her in surprise.

Not long after the twins started school, Teri and John had signed up for a dance class at the Community Centre: Marjorie had taken the twins overnight, in exchange for Teri taking Michael and Ruth the following night. What had been meant as a kind of date night, a way to reconnect after the strains and stresses of work and parenting twins, had turned into a passion for both of them. John had been really good at it, of course. He had been an athlete at school — so impressive to watch — and in dancing he found an outlet for his energy and perfectionism. Teri hadn't been as good; she always felt that she didn't have much energy left by the evenings, but she'd worked hard and learned a lot. She and John had worked towards competitions and had, finally, won one. John had been over the moon, feeling validated; Teri mostly relieved that she hadn't let him down again. And here was the proof. First Place, John and Theresa Hardy, 15 September 1973. This trophy had taken pride of place in their living room for years, where all visitors could see. Something important and real and valuable they'd done together, as a couple.

A year later, John won again, but this time with a different partner. Teri stopped doing the dance classes when Marjorie moved away and couldn't babysit, and there were always single women hoping to partner with men as good as John.

He'd always denied that there was anything between him and Betty, or Tilly, or Maggie. They were just dancing partners, people he could compete with while his wife was too busy at home, but Teri had known the truth. Too often a competition meant having to stay overnight in a hotel somewhere, even when it was only half an hour's drive from home, and she'd found receipts sometimes in his suits or in the car afterwards. Double rooms, two breakfasts, more drinks than he'd have on his own. And as time went on, he'd have 'competitions' on weekends when she hadn't seen any advertised. She couldn't confront him about it, not properly, because of the twins, and she'd convinced herself to be happy that he always came home to her, no matter how pretty or slender or talented the women he danced with.

He must have taken the trophy in the divorce, because Teri couldn't imagine giving it away if she'd had it. Why would anyone want a trophy with someone else's name on it? Except as a prop in a play, where none of the audience could see the engraving: it would be fine for that. She'd been so proud of herself, and John. It had meant so much. But of course John had taken it — dancing was his thing, not hers, and when he'd died and Sarah and Joe cleared out the house, it wouldn't have occurred to them that their mother might have wanted it. Not after the lingering bitterness of the divorce. It was an odd coincidence to see it here, that was all. All these familiar things might have come from John's house, that had once been hers too, bought by the Drama Society from whichever charity shop the twins had donated them to.

Shelving such familiar items was bittersweet, as if Teri was putting away those parts of her life. Silly to feel that way, when most of these had gone from her life decades ago, but the memories were still clear and meaningful. More clear than the play she'd just finished, somehow. What had it been called? Time of My Life, or had that been the one before? Why couldn't she remember? She couldn't even remember the name of her character. Somehow in the exhaustion after the run of performances every part she'd ever done was blending in her mind. Rosie, or Doris, or Eveline, or Agnes? Jin and Charis and Iyabo and Aedyth were all too far back. What had it been about? All she could think about, seeing these props, was her own life, the story of the play entwined with her memories.

"I'm sorry, I need more air," she said to Elizabeth. "I'm still too tired to focus."

"Go and help clear the rest of the backdrops," suggested Lizzie. "Maybe the movement will help. I can box these all up, they just need labels."

"I'm sorry, I did tell you I'd help with this."

"You've helped a lot. Just tell me, there's nothing you want to take with you?"

"No, I don't need more stuff. Memories are nice, but you don't need stuff for them. And they'll always be here to return to."

"If you can find the ones you want," said Lizzie. "You've done more parts than most, haven't you?"

"I have been around for a long time," said Teri, slightly confused. Lizzie had been in the Society longer than she had, surely? Though it was true she wasn't always on stage. Or was she thinking about June who usually managed props for their shows? When had Elizabeth joined and why did she know her so well, when she couldn't remember her ever having worked on a show before?

Shelving for the props extended in all directions, towering high above them and stretching into the dark recesses of the cavernous room, until Teri blinked and was back in the small back room with its single shelving unit, covering the entirety of two walls but no more. Most props were donated temporarily and taken back by their owners at the end of the run. Goodness knows what that glimpse of something larger had been — her eyes playing up, or maybe she'd fallen asleep for a minute. Her mother would have worried about it: "Go to the doctor, it could be a brain tumour!". Dad would have told her to get her eyes checked. John would probably have said she was fantasising.

Barney and Chris had cleared away the beach backdrop and were rolling up one that looked like a schoolroom, the bottom end of a painted blackboard just disappearing. That wasn't something Teri wanted to get nostalgic about. Neither the school she'd worked in after John, trying to earn a little extra to top up the very inadequate alimony he paid her, nor the schools the twins had attended, nor her own childhood schools, had left memories worth bringing up. She'd made friends, of course, but her memories of her friends were mostly from coffee shops, and playgrounds, and taking the children to play at houses that were always more beautifully decorated than hers. In fact, the backdrop still hanging could represent those memories: a café exterior with painted awnings to one side and a park next to it. This place was also extremely familiar, a representation of a popular local café that their audience would also have recognised. Chris was really good at backdrops, the Society was lucky to have him.

Just for a minute, she was confused again. It was a woman who led the painting for the Society scenery: Tasha, a tall woman with three children who would run around the hall while she painted; and she was assisted by a very fat man called Aris who had a booming laugh you could hear from anywhere in the building. Where did Christopher fit in? She'd known him for years, and Barnabas too, but not from the Amateur Dramatic Society. She had strange, double memories: Chris and Barney setting up and breaking down for shows, but not for the Society. So many plays, going back centuries — but that was silly, it couldn't be right.

Maybe Mum had been right. She should see a doctor. After all, she was getting on a bit, over ninety, and it wasn't surprising that she'd get a bit confused from time to time.

"Are you OK?" asked Barney. "You're looking a bit dazed. It's taking you a bit longer to come back to us, this time, isn't it? This last role took it out of you more than usual."

"I'm fine," said Teri, hastily. She didn't like people worrying about her. "I just need a bit more of a rest. Is there a lot to do, still?"

"We've got several more scenes to pull out and wrap up," he told her. "We haven't even got to your childhood yet."

"My childhood?"

She was even more confused. Had there been childhood scenes, at the start? Had she shared the role with someone younger? Was that why she didn't remember everything?

"Why don't you go and sit down for a bit?" suggested Chris. "You can just watch, yell if there's something you need to linger on."

Teri sat on her chair, comfortable and familiar, and watched them take down the last few backdrops. There were an unusual number hanging there, one in front of the other. Most plays the Society put on had only two or three; this time at least seven still hung at the back of the stage.

Tidying was going faster now, the two men in the rhythm of things. Each backdrop was lowered to the ground and unhooked from its suspending ropes, spread across the stage and carefully rolled up for storage. A woman she didn't recognise was sweeping the hall, which was no longer an auditorium; four more people were putting the dismantled tiered platforms and chairs away for the next time and from the adjacent bar came the sound of talking, laughter, and clinking glasses as the volunteers there emptied the dishwashers and put away all the clean glassware.

Maybe Teri should go and help them: it wouldn't be strenuous or mess with her memory since she'd never worked in the bar, and sitting like this was making her feel slightly guilty. She shouldn't be leaving everything to the young people. She didn't even feel old, right now. Only tired, confused and nostalgic. Her joints were no longer aching, which made a nice change. And her eyesight had improved since the dryness that had plagued her eyes for decades had temporarily gone. It was good to blink the fogginess from her vision, seeing clearly across the dress circle, even the decoration over the boxes on the far side in clear, sharp detail —

How embarrassing to fall asleep here, where everyone else was working and busy. Barnabas and Christopher had taken down the interior of a small semi-detached house like the one Teri and John had rented when they first married; a pub like the one John had worked in before he started University, when they'd first gone out together; the hospice where Teri's father had spent his last few months; her grandparents' little flat over the shop in Rickmansworth, not really big enough for them to host Theresa and Marjorie during the summer holidays but somehow they were squeezed in for a fortnight every year. Marjie on the trundle that, during the day, fitted under the spare bed where their cousins slept; Theresa on a folding bed that just fitted between the trundle and the window, and which sometimes collapsed while she was asleep, leaving her folded inside it until Mum got up and helped sort it out. Marjie had laughed until she couldn't breathe, sometimes, if that happened while she was awake.

Laughter echoing from the back woke her a bit more. She wasn't interested in the last few backdrops: the army base they'd lived on when she was small, and which she didn't really remember except from photos; the house where Mrs Deeping lived, who'd looked after her during the day while Mum worked, until she was old enough to look after herself; the hospital where she was born. Instead, she made her way to the Green Room at the back of the building, where the last few costumes were being ironed and hung up. Sophie and Bubbli must have taken them home and washed them overnight. Teri took over one of the ironing boards for a little while, ironing a small pile of children's clothes. The twins' christening robes; that lovely dress she'd found in a charity shop for Sarah's tenth birthday, and which had been worn to rags; Joe's favourite football shirt, always covered in mud and grass stains despite his mother's best efforts; his monkey pyjamas, which he'd have worn day and night, given the chance. Then some of her own dresses: the green cotton she'd made herself and worn for every one of John's work dos, every event and party, for years. The orange, flowered dress she'd splurged on in a vain attempt to make herself feel better, after her divorce. The pretty, blue, hand-smocked dress her mother had made her for a school friend's birthday party — the first proper party she'd been to — where Mary-Jane Allen had spilled lemonade down her skirt and Mrs Johnson had thought she'd wet herself and told her off. Her Guide uniform, second-hand but still a source of much pride.

"It was a full life," Elizabeth said to her.

"It was hard," said Teri. "We never had enough money, always scrimping and saving and making do. Living in rented flats with mouldy ceilings and peeling wallpaper and dripping taps we couldn't afford to get fixed. Always eating whatever was cheap, instead of what we wanted. I thought things would improve once John got a job at Cartwright's because he was supposed to be earning good money and kept getting promotions, but we still seemed to be poor all the time. Of course, he was spending half his salary on his other women, and his hobbies, and his car: my household allowance didn't increase much. He never wanted me to work, you know, he didn't want me to have a career that would take my attention. I'd have liked to do more than work in shops, I think, but there was no question of that when the children were small, of course. In those days married women didn't do that kind of thing. And later on, it was hard to get anything because I didn't have the experience, you know. Young women have so many more opportunities, these days."

"There are always drawbacks to any life. But it sounds as if you had a nice family."

"Oh, I did. There was always love to spare, as they say. Of course, Marjie was never the same after Michael died, she didn't really want to have much to do with us, and John — it was lovely at first, and when the twins were small. But he didn't hit me, you know. Lots of women weren't that lucky. Did you see poor Mrs Sinclair at the Christmas fundraiser, flinching when her husband raised his voice? I couldn't swear he hits her, but I'm sure she was afraid he would: it's a good thing they don't have children. John was never like that, I was never really afraid of him. Not much. Not often. He was strict with the children of course, he was a good father but strict, I expect he was good with the little ones too, with Maggie's babies, even though he was far too old really to start again with babies. That was a mistake, I think, her getting pregnant like that, but it's why he got the house when we divorced, he needed it more than I did. And the twins were so cross with him which wasn't really fair, I suppose. He was still their father, and they'd left home by then, they have their own families now. Children and grandchildren. Goodness, I don't know what's come over me, rattling away like an old woman, you can't be interested."

"That's why you're here," said Elizabeth. "It can be hard to shed the old memories, especially where there's love, and children. They're the hardest to let go of. But they're still here, always, archived safely so you can revisit them any time you're around, as you know. There isn't much left anchoring you to your past."

Teri looked around the vast room; racks of costumes from past roles, all neatly sorted in order, sparking memories she hadn't thought of in years.

"I just need a good rest," she said. "I think I'm worn out. I'm too old to keep doing this, one role after another."

"You won't always be," said Elizabeth. "I remember reaching that stage myself, a few centuries ago. Too many roles and no time between. But you know you're always ready for the next one, whenever the Director chooses you."

"He'd like to speak to you now, if you're ready," said Gabriel. "I don't know if it's just to debrief, or about another role, but He's waiting."

"Good luck," Elizabeth said, embracing her. "Maybe the next one will be easier."

Teri followed Gabriel to where the Director was waiting in the wings, looking out at the new set being built.

"Theresa," He said. "That wasn't an easy part for you, was it?"

"No, Sir," she said, not daring to look at His glorious face.

"You deserve to take it easy for a little while," He said. "I have a perfect role for you. You've had several in a row which have been hard work and poverty. How would you like something more upmarket? Money, society, class?"

"It could be fun," said Teri. "It would certainly make a nice change, and a change is as good as a rest."

"Lovely. It's starting a bit earlier than they expected, but I think you're about ready. There's just that chair."

Teri looked past the hospital set into the auditorium, where a new audience was filing into the gilded chairs, an expectant hush filling the plush theatre despite the sounds of musical instruments being tuned in the orchestra pit. Her old, broken down chair, loved by so many generations, looked tatty and out of place next to the red velvet and gold brocade of the auditorium, the lovely dresses and suits and fur coats of the gathering audience.

"I think I'm done with it," she said. "I doubt Joe or Sarah will want it, they don't have the memories that go with it."

"The memories they will have may not be as pleasant as yours," said the Director.

"No-one wants the chair their mother died in," said Gabriel. "We'll put it in the archive with the rest."

Teri stared at him, the final remnants of her confusion clearing away as Barnabas and Christopher, between them, carried the chair to the archive.

"They're waiting for you on stage," said the Director. "This is your cue."

"But I don't have a script," said Teri, in sudden panic. "How will I know what to do?"

"No-one knows, at the start," said the Director. "You'll pick it up as you go along. Have a lovely life, my dear. And I'm sorry about the drawbacks."

She wanted to ask him what he meant by 'drawbacks', but Gabriel was pushing her onto the stage, the spotlight, shining off his wings, dazzling her and shrinking her consciousness down to fit her new role, unaware of anything except strange hands pulling her from the warm familiar darkness into the bright cold space she couldn't properly focus on, voices making sounds which soothed her, though she didn't understand the words.

"Well done, Mrs Sinclair. You have a beautiful baby girl."

I AM STRONG
BY ALEXANDRA DIACONESCU

Red lipstick and perfume
Hair looks nice
But it's not bushed.

It all seems fine.
But what's behind that mask of mine,
It's something else I feel inside

I take a bath
It's hot
And cold.
I have visions
Of what's gone.

Screaming
Naked here,

Help!
Help me please!
But nobody's here with me.

Am I happy all alone?
I am not?
But never-mind,
I carry on!

I slip through foam
Of shower cream
And I land here.

It's all dark
I can't breathe
I feel the walls
Crushing me.
Weighing heavy on my body
Feeling bones breaking apart.

I am strong.
I am strong!
But for how long?

Then I dig a hole
I find way out.
I slide

Through mud
And rocks
And sticks
It's funny
I carried all of these.

Slide in a well
And here I am
So lost
I have never been.
Confused

And weak
I need to eat!
But it cost too much
Too much of time
So many things I could get done.

And then
Finally
I break free.

I am free!
But it's not me!

A FRESH START

BY EMILY SIGGERS

Birdsong was muffled, obscured by the thick glass windows, making its way through the vents and long twisting metal pipes. It was distorted, making the lows and highs of the tune dance together as if in a ballroom.

The faint sounds of vehicles driving by added to the cacophony; the thumping noise going over a bump in the road, the occasional 'ting!' as an errant rock hit the side of the car. The distant sounds of barking dogs and bird screeches came from over the hills, rolling over until it met me.

I was used to it - the temporary respite I was granted when the seals were broken was enough to satiate my desires to hear the outside. I sometimes wondered what would have happened if my home was different, if the path in life was chosen by someone else. Would I have moved by now?

My thoughts were broken by the light sound of a button being pressed and the clank of the gears changing as the vehicle was unlocked and alarms disarmed. I waited with bated breath, looking forward to the rush of smells and sounds once the door was opened.

I heard muffled shouts from outside, though I couldn't make out what they were saying. The voice closest to me was lower and deeper, a gruff voice that I recognised as Sam's, even through the distortion.

The outside world flooded in as one of the rear doors opened. One of the singing birds was close by, screaming words that I couldn't understand at the top of its lungs. It seemed to be effective, another bird joining it soon after and accompanying it in song. I heard the soft pitter patter of feet on the metal roof, flying off as Sam shooed them from on top of the car.

Heavy bags were loaded across the seats, the occasional clinking of metal as the bags and objects ran over the unplugged seat belts.

"Brooke!"

Brooke was the name of the woman who was often with him. She was a lot more gentle than Sam, always accompanied with an aroma of the flowers I'd once smelt on a long road trip to the coast. The perfume was a gift from Sam for their two-year anniversary - I had heard her excitedly telling a woman called Mum - and she had worn it every day of the three years since. Whether it was night or day, whether Sam was with her or not, she smelled exactly the same.

There was a dull thud as the boot opened, followed by another as a heavy object was dumped in the gap. I could hear the clinking of glass bottles, placed carefully in the holder that I assumed was in there. I'd obviously never seen it, but once bottles were put in the boot, there wasn't the telltale rolling sound that I'd heard from bottles in the backseat. More things were piled on top, the car groaning as the wheels creaked under the unexpected weight.

"Brooke, we need to go!" Sam shouted again, the annoyance and urgency evident in his voice. I heard a faint reply from the house, but it was too far away for me to hear properly. Sam was evidently able to; I could hear his loud sigh even from the other side of the vehicle.

"You said that twenty minutes ago." He said under his breath, his heavy footsteps thudding loudly on the brick floor of the driveway. The glovebox opened, the small groan of the hinges almost undetectable to the human ear. I heard him rustling through paperwork, grabbing handfuls of empty sounding plastic packets and shoving them elsewhere. Pages were leafed through, the soft echo of each page falling onto the next. Seemingly satisfied with the result, Sam put the pages back into the glovebox, the familiar creak and thud as it was closed.

He sat in the passenger seat, the quiet sound of his trousers brushing up against the leather. He leaned back with a slight groan, and a click sounded as he got out his phone, unlocking it.

"Breaking news-" The words shut off almost immediately as Sam closed the app, a silence ringing out as he checked something on his phone. He sighed quietly, shifting uncomfortably in his seat.

Random clips of songs started to play from the device, stopping and starting with the sound of his thumb tapping on the screen, his laugh sounding at different moments. Certain songs repeated over and over again, the lyrics cutting off mid word and repeating from the start.

At times the song cut out entirely for a few seconds, pierced instead by Sam muttering under his breath as he typed out words. It was a habit he did often on his own, and I enjoyed hearing what he was sending his friends from the outside.

Thought. Of. You.

Next. Boys. Trip?

Us.

Oh. My. God. Have. You. Seen. This?

We're. Going.

The last song stopped suddenly, the very slight echo reflecting quickly around the car as Sam locked his phone.

"Hey, you're finally ready." He said to someone outside, trying unsuccessfully to hide his exasperation at how long he'd been waiting.

"I said I was ready," Brooke was much closer now, her footsteps only just making noise on the brick driveway. She pulled a wheeled suitcase behind her, the wheels skipping every other step and jumping up to be pulled over. She seemed a lot more tense than she normally did; her tone seemed a lot more blunt than I was used to.

"I know." Sam replied in an equally blunt tone. There was a tension between the two of them that hung heavy in the air, words seemingly unspoken that neither of them would speak.

They stood there for a moment, breath catching every so often. Brooke coughed and sniffed, the sound reminding me of the time that she sat in the driver's seat, sobbing after the news of someone called Dad.

"Did you check the tyre pressure?" She asked, some words catching slightly before they broke through. I heard the rustle of a sleeve before the loud sound of Brooke blowing her nose.

"Yes," Sam seemed annoyed at the question, "I just checked it. All good."

"And everything else?"

"Yes!" Sam raised his voice for a moment before lowering it just as quickly, "I checked everything. Let me take your bag, you sit."

Sam stood up, a slight uncaptured groan escaping from his lips. The escapee elicited a slight laugh from Brooke as they passed each other on her way to take over Sam's seat, the waft of her perfume floating towards me.

"Shut up," Sam's tone had lightened now, a playful tone in his voice, "You're dating an old man now."

"Don't I know it." Brooke shot back, a tinkly, almost musical laugh under her breath as she pulled the passenger side door closed. I heard the soft thud of her handbag hitting the footwell, the click of it opening as she pulled out a few items.

The backseat door slammed closed, the noises within the car seeming louder without the raucous noise of the outside world.

"Hey, Rosie."

She always greeted me when she entered the car, sometimes accompanied by a soft touch causing me to move around as if in the breeze afterwards. I'd never been given a name before, or even paid attention to. I was here for a job and I did it well - or at least, I used to. As long as I was still here, that wouldn't be changing. My heyday was well over, but we had a connection and I had a feeling that I would be here for many days to come.

The tap tap of fingers texting was always absent from Brooke's messages - she much preferred sending voice notes and asking the polite sounding robot to send messages for her. It was a habit that Sam hated, but I loved hearing about all her adventures. It was a nice contrast to the quiet moments of the time sitting on the driveway.

"We're about to leave." She spoke into her phone, the familiar ding at the start and end as the message sent over to its recipient. She locked the phone with a click and I heard the sound of fabric shifting in the footwell as it was tucked away.

The boot shut with a slam and the car shook for a moment, the gears and loose metal hitting each other as the vehicle steadied itself. I could hear Sam's footsteps coming towards the driver's side, one of his hands tapping the side of the vehicle in a jaunty melody. He was always tapping something; the steering wheel, his legs, the gear stick when he was changing gears. It was sometimes in a rhythm I recognised, copying whatever was from the radio or from the music echoing tinnily through the speakers of an old phone. Sometimes it was just his own internal rhythm, a random tune he'd thought of. These were usually shortly followed with the rustling of paper, a scratchy biro scrawling a written record of what his mind had produced.

He was an aspiring musician, something he told anyone who would listen. He travelled with me to gigs, often alone but at times with a very full car of fellow band members. I could never tell who exactly was talking when they were all in together, their voices flipping around and being thrown from each side of the space until they centred on me. Depending on where we parked, I was able to hear the concert itself. The mix of the artist singing and the concert goers singing along was a joy that I couldn't describe.

My favourite concert was one that was performed from the back of someone's car, everyone playing their instruments right next to me. The door was even open, allowing me to fully experience the feeling for the first time. The vibrations itself even moved me, flying around in the wind like I was about to blow away, trapped forever in that envelope of time.

Back in the car and out of my past reminiscences,

Sam had sat down in the driver's side, adjusting the seat distance to better suit his height. He was a different height than Brooke, constantly having to readjust the seat once she'd driven it somewhere.

"Brooke," The exasperated tone was back, "Can you please put the seat back when you use it?"

"Fine, fine." There was a small waft of air as she waved her hand in his direction.

"You always say that." Sam muttered and I heard Brooke shift in her seat, seemingly about to say something but choosing to stay silent.

"Got everything?" Sam asked, turning the key in the ignition. The car came to life, the engine vibrating with a soft shuddering hum.

"Yes." Brooke was short with him, her tone not friendly. Her phone pinged with a new message tone, and she shifted again to pull it out.

An alert noise started sounding from the dashboard, but was immediately stopped by a twist and a click. A rhythmic chiming noise began as Sam turned the steering wheel to the side, his feet dancing clumsily between the pedals. The car groaned for a moment as it was pulled from its hibernating spot on the drive. The rocks shifted beneath the wheels as it moved, before steadying and sinking slightly into the road.

"Our ETA is three hours." Brooke spoke monotonously into her phone, sending the message out to whoever the recipient was.

"You know, you have fingers." Sam shot at her, his voice bouncing on the front window and reflecting as he watched the road. Brooke didn't reply, the aforementioned fingers being used to type something into her phone.

"At the end of the road, turn right onto Rose Road." The artificial voice of the navigation system echoed around the car and Sam followed the directions, the bags in the boot and backseat shifting to the other side with a crunch. One of the bottles made a high-pitched clinking noise as something passed it on its way to the floor.

The engine revved as the gears were changed, the soft but familiar stopping and starting as the stick was moved about. Sam was very familiar with this car, having owned it far longer than I'd been here for. It was his very first car, something he'd apparently fully decked out with accessories and decorations. At one point, I had someone else placed next to me, the scent of berries and mint pressing into me at times. It was overpowering, enveloping me in the strong scents for days on end. I wished then that I could speak, telling it that it was too much, that it needed to relax for a minute. It didn't seem to work immediately, but the scent faded with time before they disappeared completely. Would that happen to me someday? Outlive my usefulness and then leave to go somewhere else?

The car shook slightly as they continued driving and I could hear a metallic high-pitched noise as - what I assumed was - some loose bolts within the engine hitting each other. Every so often, the entire car jolted upwards for a moment, coming back down with a dull thud. It was repeated shortly afterwards as the back wheels went over the bump.

Sam was in the bad habit of going over these far too fast, the car coming off the road for a moment far too long, coming back down to the ground with a crunching sound that any other time would represent some major damage or destruction. When Sam was alone, he'd always laugh, the keyrings on the keys bouncing up and hitting the steering wheel like it was trying to escape the links.

He tried more when he was with Brooke, driving much less like a boy racer - a term that Mum always said with disdain anytime there was a loud car booming its exhaust as it raced on by. He'd driven Mum a couple of times, along with someone called Charlotte, though she never spoke.

There was a chiming noise again, same as when Sam first turned on the engine.

"Was that another error message?" Brooke asked,

her seat shifting and her voice moving closer to where Sam was sat.

"Nah," Sam replied, shutting off the pinging noise with a click and a twist, "It's nothing."

"It wouldn't be nothing," she huffed, returning back to her seat with a thump, the seatbelt contracting once again, "Error messages don't just show up for no reason."

"Brooke," Sam snapped back at her, before rethinking his tone for the second part of his sentence, "Sorry, but I know the car a little better than you. Just chill out."

The slight squeak that came out of Sam's mouth once the words exited his mouth revealed his regret at his words - I had only heard him tell her to 'chill' a few times and it never ended well.

"Chill?" Brooke's tone was offended, a long pause after her question.

"You know what I mean," Sam scrambled to defend himself, "Just relax, read a book. Maybe save your battery?"

"There is so much to organise," Brooke seemed to be placated by his response, tapping on her phone, "Did you have a look at anything I sent you?"

"Sure," His tone was dismissive, "But I don't think we have much choice."

"We have to make *some* good of the situation."

There was silence after her comment, only broken by the crooning of the singer quietly on the radio and the directions of the directional system. Sam coughed, the awkwardness permeating the air so much that even I could feel it.

"I'll take a look later."

"Sure." Brooke didn't seem convinced, and I was inclined to agree.

The journey continued as before, though it was much smoother than the corners and bumps of the roads in the town where they lived. I could hear the familiar racing noises of cars going far too fast, the occasional bump as they drove over a divot in the road.

It reminded me of a time when one of these rocks once hit the windscreen right next to me, accompanied with a scream and a lot of swearing from Brooke who was driving at the time.

The car had been stuck for hours after that, waiting on the side of the motorway for the repairman to come and fix it. I had a rare outing when he arrived, Brooke cradling me in her arms like a newborn baby.

"Don't want to risk you, Rosie." She told me as they waited for the repair to be completed.

The car sped up as Sam joined the motorway, the whirring noise as he accelerated more and more to join the rest of the speeding motors. There was a break every few seconds, the gap getting larger and larger as he went faster. The vehicle began to shake slightly as it reached the highest speeds - as it always did - the keychains on the car keys jostling against each other.

"Can you slow down a bit?" Brooke asked, the sound coming out slightly strained. The seatbelt stretched as Brooke tightened her hands on the belt, a habit she did often.

"I'm doing seventy, in a seventy." Sam's response was curt, flicking the indicator and turning more sharply than usual. The car shuddered as it settled back into the right direction, the noises of motors on either side rising and falling as the cars drove by us.

"This car can't cope with seventy anymore."

"At least how you drive it." Sam muttered under his breath, something that Brooke thankfully didn't seem to hear, or at least never mentioned. Still, Sam seemed to listen to her, the shuddering of the car reducing as the speed lowered.

"Thank you." Brooke's tone was quiet and bounced off the side window and back again. She seemed almost sad, like his response wasn't what she wanted.

There was a stony silence between them, though it wasn't all unpleasant. At times, it was permeated by the sound of rustling packets and handing of snacks between the two. I could always tell what side was eating what snacks - Sam gravitated towards the crunchier ones and Brooke the sour, her face crinkling with every bite, something Sam always mentioned in amusement when his attention wasn't on the road.

"Are we going to talk about it, at all?" Brooke's question was so quiet that I could barely hear it over the sound of the engine. She cleared her throat uncomfortably, the rustle of snack packets being tucked back into something in the well of the passenger side. There was no response for a moment, and I thought that Sam hadn't even heard.

"I don't know what there is left to talk about." He replied bluntly, shifting to the right and overtaking a very loud car on the left.

"Sam, you can't keep avoiding it. We need to do something-"

"Later." Sam interrupted her with a tone that left no room for argument. Brooke stopped her sentence abruptly, the last sound of a missing word falling heavily between them.

"Don't look at me like that." Sam's words were evidently accompanied by a pointed look, something that Brooke hated, "You keep saying later and later."

"I'm driving, Brooke."

"It's the motorway!" Brooke was almost shouting now, "It's one straight fucking line."

Sam didn't reply.

The radio crooned between them, breaking the awkward silence.

Who are we foolin'?
'Cause baby, we're running out of time
Didn't even know it
We just knew there was a climb

***

A dozen songs later, they finally left the motorway, tick-tocking the way to the left and sharply braking as the car drove harshly to the left.

"Take the exit at junction 8," the familiar navigator voice chimed, "In a quarter of a mile, at the roundabout, take the second exit onto Kinsley Bypass."

"Red light." Brooke said quickly, the words stumbling out of her mouth as she rushed to say it.

The car screeched to a stop quickly, the brakes and metal squealing as if the metal itself was sheering. The items in the back shifted forward with a thud, the crunching and crashing of multiple things bunching together would have made anyone wince.

The two passengers also shifted forward with the sudden stop, seat belts stretching and clicking as they prevented them from moving any closer to the dashboard of the car. They landed back in their seats with a thump.

Brooke let out a pained yelp, readjusting herself in her seat as Sam did the same.

"Thanks." She said sarcastically, her tone annoyed.

"I saw it." Sam protested, pulling the handbrake with a stretching noise. The engine noise dulled to a quiet hum as he moved the gear stick and the pedal underneath his foot was released.

"Sure." Brooke's tone remained unconvinced.

They didn't speak as they waited for the light to change, the silence only being broken by the tick-tock of the indicator. It felt almost like a countdown to something, ticking down the time they had left to make a decision on this big issue hanging over each of their heads. Something that Sam was running from and Brooke was there to pull him back to it.

"When, Sam?" Brooke asked, the words seeming to get stuck in her throat as she asked it.

Sam paused before replying.

"When, what?"

"Don't act stupid, my love." Brooke brushed her hand through her hair, the length landing noisily on her shoulders, "You've been avoiding it all week. I wanted to leave."

"Brooke," Sam said softly, as if he was about to deliver bad news, "I can't right now."

Brooke let out an exasperated sigh.

"Look," she tried to say as kindly as she could, "I know you didn't want to leave. But I really think-"

"Lights have changed!" Sam interrupted her to exclaim, the engine turning on to full volume as Sam moved back into gear. The car started with a jolt, followed by a cacophony of others surrounding them moving forward at the same time. There were some honks of car horns and repeated beeps as some of them danced with each other. I liked to imagine that they each had their own version of me with them, hearing the world as it flew beside. Maybe some of them had travelled, gone between cars with different owners as they, or their cars, passed over to the other side.

Brooke stayed silent as the vehicle left its turning, the steering wheel spinning around as if in a race car. The car felt like it was going to tip over for a second, stretching as the wheels locked in place to make the angle. It was a feeling that I loved; it never failed to move me around, twisting and dancing with the wind whistling through the small gaps in the doors. I felt free, especially when the windows were opened and the danger of being whisked out of the open world just inches away.

The navigation system spit out a 'ba-dink' error noise as it tried to figure out a new route to their destination.

"Continue on Thistle Way for fifteen miles." It sputtered out.

"Sam!" Brooke chastised him, "You've added so much time to the journey."

I could almost hear her gritted teeth, but she bit her tongue.

"I know what I'm doing."

Brooke scoffed, but didn't say anything else to Sam.

"We're going to be late," Brooke spoke into her phone, the familiar monotone voice that accompanied her voice notes, "Maybe thirty minutes?"

"Brooke." Sam said, his tone much less avoidant this time, "I love you, but-"

He paused for a second and there was a shifting noise as he moved his arm.

"I don't know," he continued, "I still think leaving was the wrong decision. It's too soon."

"You heard what happened with the-" Brooke choked up for a moment, coughing to clear her throat, "You know it was the right decision."

"We left, didn't we?" Sam's words were blunt

once again, firm, but I could tell he was trying to keep his tone neutral and calming.

"I know," Brooke replied quietly, every breath taking longer as she tried to steady her shaking breaths, "It's still hard, our life was-"

"Sam!" she screamed suddenly, cutting herself off mid-sentence, "The road!"

"Shit!" Sam swore loudly as he slammed his foot on the brake, the car screeching as it tried to stop its forward movement in an instant. I waved around the cockpit, twisting and turning so fast I thought that I would fly out of the window if it were open. I could hear both of them brace themselves against the seats, Brooke's fingernails scratching over the hard plastic in a desperate attempt to avoid the impact.

But it was too late. I could hear the muffled screeching of metal as the car made contact with whatever was in the road. It was accompanied by a loud thud, shortly followed by a crash and crack as the object made contact with the windshield. Brooke screamed again as she was thrown forward into the breaking glass, her seatbelt straining the hardest it ever had to stop her from moving out through the windscreen.

"Brooke!" Sam shouted, the lurching and crashing almost fully obscuring the noise even as he tried to rise above it. She didn't seem to hear him, landing back on the seat with a thump as the car came to a stop. The object flew past the windscreen, hitting the roof several times before it thudded dully somewhere behind the vehicle.

It was only a few seconds between Sam pushing hard on the brakes and actually stopping, but it felt like it had lasted for hours. The silence in the car was only broken by the sounds of heavy breathing and the quiet voice on the radio reading out the headlines as quickly as she could.

--officials warn to stay away from–

The radio cut off with a click.

"What-" Brooke's voice was shaky, words unsure even as they were leaving her lips, "...was that?"

"You okay?" Sam asked, worry leaking into his voice.

"Yeah," Brooke winced, "Just a bit sore from the seatbelt. You?"

Sam didn't reply, the sound of jingling as his hands shook trying to turn the car key. The engine shut off with a click, the sudden cut off feeling jarring even after the sudden impact. They both sat there in silence, the tap tap of Sam's fingers on the leather of the steering wheel piercing the silence.

"Sam, we have to…" she seemed unsure how to continue, "We have to check."

"No," his voice was unsettled but he seemed a lot

more sure of his words than Brooke was, "Brooke, we can't."

"What if it was a person?"

"What if it wasn't?" Sam's voice was unsteady, the sound quivering and warping as it made its way over to Brooke. It was a tone I'd never heard from him before, his voice being almost painful to get out of his mouth.

Brooke's hands fumbled as she took off her seatbelt with a loud click and tapped on the door as she quickly opened it, the desperation making her miss the handle a few times. The door swung open, the hinges whining as it was pushed to its furthest opening and tried to go further. There was a quiet tinkling noise as shards of glass fell from her lap onto the ground.

"Brooke!" There was the sound of falling pocket contents as Sam lunged unsuccessfully to grab her before she left. He collected himself back into his seat, leaving the stuff that had fallen out of his pockets spayed around the car and clicked his own seatbelt off, the whirring of the belt moving back into its original position echoing around as if in a slow-motion movie.

I could hear Brooke's footsteps as she carefully but quickly retreated to the back of the car, where the object had fallen. I couldn't hear what it was, the only sounds that came from it being from the impact. Could it have been a person? I would have assumed that they would have made more noise, groaning in pain as they laid on the floor. Were they dead?

Hopefully it was a random object or even an animal instead. We'd hit an animal once before, a bird that chose the worst possible place to take a break. I'd heard the impact, as well as the crunch as the poor thing was pulled below the car. The stop was similar to this, sudden with a moment to breathe before any action.

It was both of them that time, Brooke almost inconsolable when she'd figured out what they had done. It was a bloody scene, she had screamed about it, but there wasn't anything that anyone could do. Sam was much calmer then, reassuring Brooke with some kind words and holding her as she cried.

"Brooke, keep your distance!" he shouted now, opening the door and throwing it open in the same fashion that she had a few seconds beforehand. Both doors were kept wide open, the outside world that I so loved was flooding in at a fast pace. Any other time, I would be revelling in the sounds coming in, considering every leaf fall and insect buzz. Today, though, I was concentrating on the two figures who were investigating what they had hit.

Brooke's breath stopped for a split second as she softly gasped.

"Sam," she said in a whisper that I could hear from the other side of the vehicle, "It's a dog."

"Brooke," Sam's tone was almost begging now, his whisper moving down as he cautiously followed Brooke to where she was standing, "We have to leave it. You heard what they said on the news."

"But, Sam…" she dawdled for a moment, her voice the most unsure I'd ever heard it, "It's just a dog."

"You know what happened to the Allens." Sam pressed her again, his voice almost at his normal speaking volume, "Please, love, get back in the car."

Brooke didn't reply but I could hear a step as she rocked back and forth, debating internally as she fought different sides. She was a massive animal lover, always showing Sam clips with barking animals and pointing out every time she saw one as they drove by it. They'd had a tough conversation on the way home one day about having their own pet, something that wasn't allowed where they currently lived, but even I knew that she was desperate to have one of her own one day.

It was the reason for the argument that she was having to fight herself on at the moment, the animal lover versus listening to the love of her life.

"Please, let's leave." Sam seemed slightly calmer now, something having changed between the two that I missed from my position in the front to the car. Brooke sniffed, a mucus-y sounding noise that I knew meant that tears were streaming down her face.

"Let's just go." She said quietly, her footsteps beginning to softly patter back to her seat in the car. Sam started moving too, his hands steadying himself as he quickly but carefully made his way back to the seat. They both paused before they got back, hands on the roof just outside of the entrance back to the safety of the vehicle.

The next few minutes played out in slow motion, lasting hours but also over in an instant.

Sam screamed Brooke's name and she turned, her back hitting the open passenger car door.

A snarl unlike anything I'd heard before, a warning before the moment.

She screamed, the growls of the dog muffled as it latched onto some appendage or side. The noise pulsated as she tried to shake it off, loud thuds sounding as she hit everywhere she could reach.

Sam climbed through the car, turning the key at the driver's seat before trying to grab Brooke towards him. His flailing arms hit different parts, different sounds ringing out as he hit solid and hollow surfaces.

The dog let go with a yelp, Brooke falling with a crunch into the passenger's seat. Her screams were only punctuated by impacts as she kicked at the animal, hitting it with a sickening sound every other hit.

The car started to accelerate away, Sam now back in the driver's seat. The engine revved as he struggled to change gear quickly enough.

The door closed with a metallic slam, the locks engaging the second it did. The beeping noise stopped quickly afterwards, being replaced with a different tone.

The car continued to speed along, navigating skilfully through twists and turns.

It felt like an age before Sam spoke.

"Where?"

"My arm." Brooke sobbed quietly, pained noises escaping through gritted teeth. Sam's hands gripped the wheel tighter, the leather straining under his fingertips so much it felt like it would almost split. Neither spoke again for some time, the silence breaking from the sounds of the engine turning and speeding up as he drove away from the scene of the crime.

The chiming noise started up again, joining the other tone, but neither seemed to notice this time. It repeated over and over again, never changing tone or speed. Eventually, the noise seemed to stop on its own.

"What do we do?" She asked, pained gasps coming out between each word.

"I don't know." Sam's tone was strange, his voice sounding like it was coming from somewhere else. If I didn't know that there wasn't anyone else in the car, I wouldn't have recognised it. It was almost cold, distant. It wasn't something that I'd ever heard him like.

"I'm sorry, love," Brooke was in tears, shifting in her seat and stretching the seatbelt as she turned to face Sam.

"I told you to leave it." Sam's tone was still cold.

"It was just a dog," she rushed to try to justify herself, pausing at points where the pain in her arm overwhelmed her, "I didn't think it was a big deal."

"Have you even listened to the news?"

Brooke hesitated for a moment, starting a few words and stopping before any of them finished themselves. Sam responded by turning the radio on, flicking between each channel so it spoke like a highlights reel.

"...animal attacks rise across the country..."

"...after the death of thirteen people in a zoo on Monday..."

"Officials advise residents to shelter in place where possible…"

"…shelters and hospitals are overwhelmed…"

"The government announces new measures to tackle the rise in abnormal animal activity…"

The last word was stopped as the radio clicked off, echoing around us. There was no response from Brooke at first, just a soft crying sound emanating from the passenger side of the car.

"Sam, please look at me." The seatbelt on Sam's side stretched as he shook his head, his grip tightening even more on the steering wheel.

The chiming was back again, the sound piercing the quiet like a heartbeat. Brooke clicked her seatbelt back in and it dulled for a moment before returning with an increased frenzy.

Sam tried to kill it with the familiar turn and click sound, but it started back up again almost as quickly. It seemed to get faster until it was almost on top of itself, the heartbeat increasing as the tension rose within the vehicle.

"What on earth is that beeping?"

"It's nothing." Sam tried unsuccessfully to turn off the chiming, speeding up as the clicks and turns became more aggressive. The car wobbled as it turned around a corner, but it didn't stop.

The car veered to the left, then to the right and

back again as it tried to gain traction. The tilting was extreme, almost feeling like it was about to tip completely over to its side. Brooke screamed, the noise becoming all too familiar. Sam didn't speak, and I could just hear the sound of the steering wheel turning in either direction, trying desperately to figure out which way the car was spinning.

The contents of the boot switched sides forcefully, banging heavily as it did. I wasn't even sure if there would be anything left when it was opened, insides spilling all over the boot. I heard a bottle smash as it hit the others, the bottom of it tumbling out of the container.

Sam's frantic turning seemed to work, the car sliding sideways in the dirt so quickly it felt like it was about to do that final step of falling. I flew around, whipping around fast around the front, but going nowhere fast.

The car jolted to a stop, shaking hard as it steadied itself. Brooke screamed once again, the seatbelt stretching as she leant forward to muffle her mouth with her hands. There was a pained gasp that joined the fray as she leant over her wounded arm. Sam didn't say anything as she threw open the passenger door at the same time as releasing the belt that was holding her down. Her footprints landed uncharacteristically noisily on the ground, a groan emanating from her mouth as she wrenched herself upwards.

"Sam." Brooke was angry, the kind of angry that I hadn't seen very often, if ever. I could almost feel the seething fury coming from her side directed at Sam.

Sam seemed startled by her anger as well, the soft fleshy sound of his mouth opening and closing like it did when he didn't know what to say.

"The. Tyres." Every word was dripped in venom; she was almost spitting. "You. Didn't. Check. The. Fucking. Tyres."

A small gasp came from Sam as his hand hit his body in exasperation.

"Shit, Brooke," he apologised, "I got caught up."

"It's not good enough!" She was still angry, her voice getting more distant as her footsteps got further away from the car. I heard a crunching thud as she sat down on some kind of rock or wall, breathing heavily.

Sam took this time to leave the vehicle himself, walking around the front of the car and crouching down with a click of his bad knee to accompany it.

"Oh, it's just a flat." He seemed relieved, with a touch of confusion in his voice, "Love, we have a spare."

Brooke just grunted in response, coming out between clenched teeth.

Sam stood up from his position by the wheel, his firm footprints shifting on the dirt from where the car had ended its spin. Brooke grunted again, like a scared dog trying to warn its attacker to stay away. It didn't take Sam long to get to her and I heard the soft sound of his hand grasping hers as she tried to shift to move away.

"Love, breathe." His voice was sweet, caring. I adored when he spoke to Brooke like this, so tender and compassionate. I didn't hear it often, just when she really needed some comfort. Like the time that the person named Dad was found, lost on the side of the road. It didn't do anything to stop her crying, but I knew that she felt like she could depend on Sam for anything. She'd told me as much, the times when she and I were alone in the car and she'd vent or gush about something he'd done the previous day.

"I don't know what's wrong with me." She cried, the sound muffled by something around Sam, likely his shirt, as she often did when she was upset. Sam didn't say anything other than a quiet shushing sound, the soft sound of hair brushing I could only just hear.

"Let me look at this bite." I heard pained noises emanating from Brooke, gritted teeth and small whimpers as Sam checked out her wound. He didn't say anything but inhaled heavily, taking a loud step back.

"You're burning up, too." His tone had changed to something that I wasn't sure if Brooke would have picked up on. I'd spent a good deal of time alone with Sam and I could tell when he was happy, excited, sad, angry. This was a tone that I didn't hear very often, only heard about when he didn't want to show his emotions to someone. Something was being hidden that he didn't want her to know about.

"I'll get the first aid kit. Can you wrap it up whilst I'm changing the tyre?"

"Okay." Brooke's voice was neutral but exhausted, the long day taking its toll on her. The boot opened and Brooke gasped quietly at the sound of objects falling to the ground. They thumped on the back of the car as Brooke or Sam attempted to catch some of their possessions, but the effort wasn't successful as the majority of things fell. I just hoped it wasn't anything too valuable.

"This is a mess." Brooke said bluntly and there was a pause before both of them laughed quietly to each other, the car shaking slightly as they steadied themselves on the chassis. It was a welcoming sound and not something I'd heard for a while. Brooke's laugh was always light like a bell chiming, tinkling at the high end like a beautiful melody. Sam's was much more gruff; except when he completely lost it and it was only the tiniest squeaks that came out of his mouth in response. Their laughs harmonised like the perfect duet, a recipe for lovely mirth that I loved to hear.

"We've got to move some bits to get to the tyre," Sam's voice was lighter, the slight hint of laughter still remaining on it, "First aid kit is there."

Brooke took something out - presumably the aforementioned first aid kit - and placed it on the ground by the back tyre. Other things were thrown out and smashed on the floor, glass bottles with liquid still remaining. There was a loud scraping noise as the contents of the boot were pulled to the side, grunts coming from Sam as he strained to get the spare tyre from its compartment in the back of the car. There was a large bang on the dirt, the tread on the tyres compacting the mud as it was rolled towards the broken tyre.

The plastic of the first aid kit cracked and strained as it was opened, the contents evidently being taken out to treat this wound of Brooke's. Sam got to work changing the tyre, the telltale sounds of the car being hiked up and the bolts being loosened.

It wasn't anything particularly interesting to listen to, so I let my focus drift to the outside world.

Sam's door had been left open, so everything was flooding in.

It was a quiet day, without the sounds of too-fast driving cars speeding by. In the distance, I heard a dog howl, a mournful noise that made me think of one of the werewolf movies I'd had the privilege of listening to during a precious drive-in cinema experience. I often thought of that film on long boring road trips, ones where I couldn't hear anything but the sound of the radio at full volume.

The animal didn't seem too close at the moment, so unlikely to pose any danger to the pair as they chatted about what they needed to do once they arrived at their destination.

Wind was blowing between the leaves of a forest or greenery that seemed to be on a different side of the road as where they had come to a stop. It danced around in the air, taking hostages of pine cones as they fell from canopies.

There was a noticeable lack of birdsong in the air, no screeching red kites or shrieking sea gulls. Thinking about it, I hadn't heard much of them at all since we had left the driveway back at home. At the time, I hadn't really thought about it, focusing more on Sam and Brooke's conversations and busy traffic. Was something else going on?

"Done." Sam had finished putting on the tyre, the

sound of creaking metal as he removed the jack from the bottom of the vehicle. Brooke let out a small cheer, closing the first aid kit and placing it in the boot of the car along with the metal jack. She closed the door with a loud thud.

"What do we do with the old tyre?"

"Just leave it at the side."

Sam made his way over to the driver's side, his body acting as a muffle and block to the wind that had softly moved me about. Brooke hesitated for a moment, her hand on the handle of the passenger seat. The window was open still, wind pushing through to Sam's body.

"I gotta pee." the car bounced slightly as she did, her fingers tapping on the window frame.

"Can you wait?" Sam seemed nervous, his fingers drumming on the gearstick like he always did. It was a tapping that seemed forced. I'd heard that noise enough times.

"No."

Sam sighed, the seatbelt stretching as he turned to look over each shoulder.

"If you go over there," he pointed in a direction outside the car, "You can't be seen from the road."

Brooke paused, hands still resting on the passenger window.

"Okay," her voice was serene, with the hint of tiredness in it, "I'll go."

She walked along the back of the car to the driver's side, pausing at the open door where Sam was sitting.

"I love you."

"I love you too."

Sam's tapping increased as I heard Brooke's footsteps fade away as she reached the forest, rustling through undergrowth for a moment before disappearing entirely after a few seconds.

Almost in sync with the final footstep that I could hear, Sam exhaled, a long drawn out breath that he seemed to have been holding for a long time. There was almost a stifled sob sound at the end of it, but Sam never cried. Brooke was always the emotional one, crying at everything from random videos on her phone or talking about some old memory. But Sam? Never. Something was very wrong.

Still sniffing, he fumbled in his pockets and I quickly heard the sound of his phone unlocking. He swiped for a moment, tapping on the screen to search for something. He didn't speak, just silently swiping and searching for something. I could hear a tiny splash hitting the screen at times, but he would just wipe his hand over the front and continue with his search.

He leant back in his seat but didn't seem to relax, a quiet thud as the phone hit the steering wheel.

"I'm here outside the Kent and Canterbury hospital, where there has been a rise in serious admissions with the so-called Feral Syndrome."

The voice was cheery, but matter-of-fact as it read out the news report, the unseen woman speaking loudly from the phone speakers.

"The Prime Minister, along with the health department, has released a set of symptoms to look out for. If you or a loved one exhibits any of these, please quarantine yourself or others to stop the illness from spreading."

"Fever."

"Check." Sam whispered, pausing the video after every listed symptom.

"Cough."

"Nope."

"Itching"

"Not that either."

"Increased aggression."

"Yes."

"Confusion."

"I guess."

"There have been unconfirmed reports that the symptoms start after an altercation with a wild animal. Stay tuned for more on this story."

The news reel ended there, but Sam swiped on

his screen to check the next video. The tone of this was one completely different, shouts and vehicles driving by were almost deafening in the background. Sirens permeated through every few seconds.

"I'm back here, outside…outside Kent hospital."

It was the same reporter from before, but her voice was different, distracted, almost scared.

"Something has happened inside the emergency department-"

Her words stopped and started, as if she was looking at something.

"Officials at the hospital have advised to stay away unless absolutely necessary-"

I could hardly hear what she was saying after a cacophony of overlapping sirens, muffled shouts from officials and a louder screaming.

"-reports of violent outbursts-"

"-attacks on staff-"

"Death occurs a day after exposure, without fail."

"Doctors are working on a cure, but people are dying faster than they can help-"

The video cut off suddenly, the screaming and shouting still echoing around me. Sam sobbed, a heartbroken almost guttural scream. He punched the steering wheel as he cried, the horn sounding every hit as if to accentuate his grief. The leather creaked, threatening to break with the weight of what he had decided.

I could hear Brooke's footsteps rushing towards the car, pausing as another motor drove by. There was a loud click and clunking as the locks engaged. The windows slid shut with a whirring noise, and Sam's phone dropped noisily to the floor.

"Love?" Brooke's question was muffled, noise obscured through the glass, "What's wrong?"

Sam turned the key, the engine coming to life.

"Sam?" The sound of the handle rattling joined Brooke's confused voice, doing nothing to unlock the car. She tapped on the glass, quiet at first and increasing in severity.

"Sam, it's not funny." She was getting angrier, but I could tell she was trying to keep everything calm, "Love, open the door."

The car was moved into gear, slowly rolling forward. Sam was silent, barely even breathing. It felt like the vehicle had a mind of its own, just running away from danger.

"Sam?" Brooke was almost running now to try to catch up, her hands desperately grasping at the handle to try to open the door. It rattled so hard it threatened to break, the tension rising.

"Sam, open the fucking car! Don't be stupid!" She was shouting now, not even trying to fight the rage that was bubbling up inside of her. She was losing pace, her hands switching between banging on the metalwork and the glass of the windows so hard it felt like it was about to break.

Her voice tuned out as floods of memories came rushing in. I knew this was goodbye.

I'd been there for all of it.

"Sam, look!" The first thing I'd heard Brooke say to me, picking me up shortly after and holding me close.

"It smells amazing."

"Where would we even put it?" Sam had asked, laughter coming into his voice as easily as a flowing waterfall. Brooke laughed in response, and it almost felt like she was putting me back before she was handing over cash to the man at the desk and I was on my way.

The car jolted, rolling over a pothole.

Their first kiss, leant into the open window as she was dropped home. A peck at first, coming back for more. She had to tear herself away, Sam driving home afterwards telling his best friend about a date with a dream girl.

Brooke was behind the car now, her fists still trying to get in somehow.

"Are you nearly done?" Brooke was moving in with Sam, the car heaving from the many trips between the two places.

"One last load, I promise." She put down a particu-

larly heavy box in the boot and there was a loud popping noise from the boot side.

"Did you break my car?"

I could still hear her screaming out the back, the noise seeming so clear even through the closed windows. I wished that I could shout back at her, some noise coming through my tattered body and saying something for the first time in my existence. But nothing came out.

"Mum says we should get out of the city, go to visit her."

"We're safe here, trust me."

"I think we should go. We're so near the Zoo."

"They've put extra protections in place."

"Sam, please." Brooke's tone was begging, her fingers scratching the sides of the door anxiously. There was a pause between the two, just listening to the radio as Sam drove.

"I'll think about it."

"Thank you, I know it's hard. I love you."

"I love you too."

Brooke's voice faded into nothingness, as if her entire being had just vanished. Sam let out the sob he'd been holding in, quietly whimpering and weeping as he drove. I heard a howling dog, the sound like a mourning bell.

"It's just you and me now, Rosie."

AFTERWORD

If you are interested in knowing more about the Herts Writing Group, we can be found on Facebook under 'The Hertfordshire Writing Group'. We are active on Discord and meet once a month online to discuss everything writing, books and everything else.

ABOUT THE AUTHORS

CALUM DICKINSON

Calum Dickinson is originally from Scotland. He has worked and lived in Hertfordshire for over a decade, training people how to use scientific equipment. From 2009, he has participated and won 16 NaNoWriMo events, creating stories ranging from Mystery, Fantasy, Steampunk and Historical. Each year he tries a new method for writing or coming up with new concepts and ideas, although puns are often the winning influence. Other than writing, he enjoys birdwatching, painting and DIY, with an interest in vintage tools. Calum can be followed on Instagram @calumbirds and YouTube @scopingouttools

TAYLOR MCLEOD

Taylor is a legal professional by day and an avid writer by night. She is a keen runner, and uses her long runs in nature as inspiration for her stories, which tend to dabble in the realm of sci-fi and fantasy, usually with a darker undertone. She joined the Hertfordshire Writing Group in 2021, after being a solo writer for most of her life, and is so proud of the different stories they have created together.

EMILY SIGGERS

Emily (Em) Siggers is an ex-teacher living in Hertfordshire with her partner of seven years, Lee. She joined the Hertfordshire Writing Group after participating in National Novel Writing Month in 2020 and has been writing with the group ever since. She mainly writes fantasy and stories within her own world of Gevola, which she has spent over 15 years creating. Other than writing, she loves anything textiles and often attends sessions with an ongoing craft or cross-stitch project. Emily can be followed on Instagram @essacharl

ALEXANDRA DIACONESCU

Passionate about sustainability, she is slowly building her path in this field. She returned to writing about two years ago and rediscovered how calming it can be. In her free time, she loves to write poetry and has also written two children's books that she hopes to publish soon.

BERNADETTE LYNN

Bernadette Lynn was born in Zambia and spent her childhood in Africa and Saudi Arabia, before moving to Hertfordshire. She studied violin making at the London College of Furniture before her marriage and has since spent several years raising and home educating her four, now adult, children.

Writing has been an interest for her since she first had a story published in the magazine for the World-wide Education Service at the age of eight. It has now become a passion and she spends far too many hours neglecting housework while writing.

CÉCILE KEEN

Cécile lives in Hertfordshire with her husband, who is not only her best writing supporter but also her volunteered appointed first and last editor. They met about 30 years ago and retired recently. Together they love travelling and touring in their beloved motorhome across the UK and Europe. Being life members of English Heritage for three decades have allowed them and their two sons, both currently university students, to enjoy countless visits and live history shows at EH properties creating wonderful family memories. Cécile is a bookworm and mostly enjoys fiction and autobiographies. She learnt crochet at a young age, though her true love is cross-stitching, especially traditional design samplers. Cécile wrote a diary during the Covid lockdown, and she has continued writing since. She usually writes short stories, inspired by world events and emotions that life takes us through.

ALSO BY THE GROUP

SNAPSHORTS:
COLLECTED STORIES

A spinster reveals that her life hasn't been as loveless as everyone thought.

A naïve photographer captures the absurd brutality of the Vietnam War.

A model's descent into darkness after a photography session at sea.

A girl. An attic. One mystery. Six photographs. A way out?

Two men. One secret. A photograph that seems to know.

A kidnapped woman has to photograph a dangerous cybertronic creature in order to win back her freedom from a greedy ruler.

From historical fiction to science fiction, mystery to romance, these unforgettable stories will linger with you long after you finish the last page.

FOLKLORE FROM THE HERTS

Have you ever wondered where the line between ancient myth and our modern world blurs? *Folklore From the Herts,* a unique anthology from The Hertfordshire Writing Group, invites you on an enchanting journey where this line not only blurs but completely vanishes. This collection is not merely stories; it's a portal to a realm where the echoes of age-old myths resonate within the rhythms of our contemporary lives.

Within these pages lies a treasure trove of tales that delve deep into the eternal experiences of love, destiny, and transformation where characters confront the legacy of their heritage, challenge long-standing beliefs, and unearth the profound influence of myths in shaping our present-day realities.

A healer facing a moral dilemma that defies ancient codes, a young woman grappling with the weight of legendary expectations, and a voice from the mystic isles calling to a chosen one. These stories, and many more, serve as a testament to the transformative power of choices and their far-reaching consequences.

From the corners of a cobwebbed attic to the hidden heart of mystical isles, *Folklore From the Herts* reveals how the most unlikely of friendships can teach us profound lessons in empathy and understanding. Each story is a mirror reflecting the unexpected connections that can dramatically alter our perceptions and guide our life's path.

This anthology redefines the ordinary, transforming everyday moments into magical experiences. It reminds us that sometimes, the most captivating stories are hidden in the simplest of places, waiting for the right eyes to uncover them.

Immerse yourself in *Folklore From the Herts* and embark on an unforgettable journey that celebrates the enduring magic of folklore. These tales are more than narratives; they are a mosaic of timeless truths and universal connections that bind us all.

9 781919 416014